I See You

I See You

Ishtiyaq Shukri

Published by Jacana Media (Pty) Ltd in 2014

10 Orange Street
Sunnyside
Auckland Park 2092
South Africa
+2711 628 3200
www.jacana.co.za

ISBN 978-4314-0875-7

Cover design by publicide
Set in Sabon 11/14pt
Job No. 002142
Printed and bound by Creda Communications

See a complete list of Jacana titles at www.jacana.co.za

For my mother, who would have travelled the road to Atouf in August 2013, before Allah called her on the ultimate journey.

And for my aunt, who continued to read the draft manuscript to her when she had become too weak to read herself.

What, then, is the 'deep state'? Here is how it works. You think your country has undergone a transition to democracy. You have had roughly free and fair elections. You have new leaders in charge. Yet you begin to realise that, as the French say, the more things change the more they stay the same. You realise there are powerful elite formations bequeathed by years, even decades, of authoritarian rule still able to block progressive change and protect their interests …

The point is this: there are deep states in many countries today. Wherever you find a newish democracy of a rough and ready sort coming out of a long period of authoritarian rule, chances are there is a deep state at work; and one determined to protect the gains and interests of those who did immensely well under authoritarian rule.

– *Sina Odugbemi*

Black Paint White Strokes

Freedom was here
We were told
She stood right there
A sight to behold
Strong and mighty
Like the Drakensberg

Did we slumber
Through the thunder
That heralded her coming?
Did we blink
And missed her mischievous wink?

Marikana tears of blood
Mourn the death of the noble tree
Killed for the beauty of her wood
Voracious white ants feast upon her
From her manicured toes
To her African button nose
Her hollow frame crumbled in fragmented dust
dreams

Familiar faces from the trenches
Turned oppressors on Parliament benches
We the people
Looked through greed's peephole
At our freedom dream
Now painted black in white strokes
Chained in familiar shackles
We have been here before

– *Abdul Milazi, 26 September 2012, following the massacre at Marikana on 16 August 2012*

OPENING SENTENCES

Atouf

Good evening from Atouf.

We, the freedom-loving young people of Palestine, are proud to initiate this relay readathon in protest against the recent abduction in South Africa of the photographer and journalist Tariq Hassan.

During the readathon, we will be reading Tariq's article on Palestine from 2006, titled '... And 1 Can of Sardines'.

Just as Tariq made his voice heard for us then, we will make our voices heard for him now. We will be reading in alternating cycles of Arabic and English. We will read in relays until Tariq is released or found. Our readathon will be streamed here, live, twenty-four hours a day.

If the freedom and liberty of journalists and writers around the world is a cause you support, we invite you to join in our reading protest from wherever you are and in whatever language you speak.

We will start reading in a few minutes, at 19.33 South African time – the exact time of Tariq's abduction in Johannesburg one month ago tonight.

The first twenty-four-hour cycle of the readathon commences here in Atouf, the starting point of Tariq's article. Thereafter, it will be taken up in

Johannesburg. Our first reader is Tariq's long-time associate and close friend here in Palestine, Yahya Al Qala'awi …

From Yahya to Leila

From: Yahya.AlQalaawi@...
To: Leila.Mashal@...
Subject: Tariq
Date: 4 July 20—

Dearest Leila,
I've just seen the news. I've been trying to call you, but keep getting your voicemail. I can't imagine what you must be going through. I'll keep trying your phone from time to time, but for now I'm just letting you know that we're working on a campaign for Tariq's freedom.

If there's anything you need, anything at all, you are not alone.
Yahya

From: Leila.Mashal@...
To: Yahya.AlQalaawi@...
Subject: Tariq
Date: 11 July 20—

Dear Yahya,
Thank you for your emails and calls. And thank you, Yahya, for always being there for us.

I'm sorry for my delayed response. Our room had also been ransacked. Tariq's computer and our cellphones were taken.

I've always feared this, given the nature of his work. Except I always imagined they'd get to him while he was away and that I would be woken in the middle of the night by a phone call from somewhere far away. I never thought that it would happen in South Africa while I was sipping champagne in a black dress and diamond pendant.

'None are more hopelessly enslaved than those who falsely believe they are free.'
Leila

Eight months later

Eroded by isolation and moth-eaten in darkness, my recollections appear only in flashes, like a burglar's torch searching the night. So start with what is happening now, it's as good a place as all the rest, midstream, with you at the kitchen table dragging this pencil across this scrap of paper. They'll figure it out. But after decades of keyboards and monitors, longhand no longer comes easily. Holding a pen for longer than it takes to sign a prescription has become an effort. Look at this scrawl. Will you be able to make sense of it in the morning? Still, such are the means at your disposal. Your computer has been confiscated. Perhaps when you come to make revisions, you'll call that plot point one. Perhaps <u>if</u> you come to making revisions ... You're not allowed to leave your house. Who knows how that will play out? You might call that plot point two, but your captors are calling it 'administrative internment'. Lovely.

I sign my name, just to keep in practice.
Leila Mashal

19.33 South African time

Following the election of Hamas in January 2006, US- and EU-led sanctions crippled the Palestinian National Authority. The political class remained in place, but what were the consequences for ordinary Palestinians already hemmed in by decades of Israeli military occupation?

'... And 1 Can of Sardines' was written by Tariq Hassan and first published in the *London Standard* on Sunday 29 October 2006. It is read tonight from Atouf by his colleague and friend Yahya Al Qala'awi, as part of a wider campaign of protest against his abduction.

The road to Atouf is narrow, no more than three metres wide, and from the nearby village of Tammoun, only eight kilometres long. You'd be hard-pressed to find it on a map. Few Palestinians travel here, and even fewer foreigners. In a country struggling with catastrophe at almost every turn, this single-width rural track is a good place to start. It winds through one of the most remote and dramatic landscapes of the stark Jordan Valley in the east of the West Bank into one of the most breathtaking panoramas in the region. This place of desolate splendour is the setting for a quiet, faraway tragedy of termination, for which Atouf's dead-end road is so precise a symbol it seems almost contrived. Having delivered the traveller to this isolated farming hamlet, the road stops suddenly beside the ruins of four Palestinian farmsteads bulldozed by the Israeli Defence Forces. Palestinians here, it seems, have reached the end of the road.

On the mountainside, dry stone walls and ancient burial sites testify to how long that road has been in existence. Today, the hamlet's 1 200 residents are being pried from their ancestral land, livelihood and way of life by organised and sustained Israeli military force. Their wells locked, they are bereft of the most crucial commodity in the region – water. Their valley now lies barren. Unable to cultivate crops, they barter their last remaining resource, their sheep, in exchange for water imported from Tammoun. Everything is on the brink. It is hard to determine what the pathetic remnants of decimated flocks, muzzles foraging through stones, are grazing upon. More than 60 per cent of farmland stretching from here to the Jordan River has been seized, a domino process of land confiscation on an unimaginable scale moving southwards, all the way to Jericho.

For a snapshot of Israel's designs for this eastern region, come to Atouf. With the Wall in the west now complete, construction in the east is set to begin. According to the Jerusalem Legal Aid and Human Rights Center, construction in the east will be swift and easy. The Wall here will stampede everything in its path and places like Atouf will simply cease to exist.

In Atouf's panorama Israel's grand scheme is plain to see. While whole swathes of the valley now lie unproductive, beyond where the road ends, on the confiscated southern slopes, Israel's project lies in full, lush bloom – vineyards flourishing in settlements irrigated by water redirected from seized Palestinian wells. But why should this concern a Londoner? Because while Palestinian farmers struggle to get their produce to the markets of Ramallah, produce from these settlements will end up in the supermarkets of the European Union – Israel's largest trading partner – whose current sanctions are driving Palestinians into deeper poverty.

Travel the road to Atouf, while it is still there. Look around the demolished homes, doors still dangling from their hinges. Survey the dry wasteland from which the wind sweeps dust into the eerily silent village school, closed since September because its teachers have not been paid for eight months. To sojourn here is to confront an incongruous irony – that such a diminutive rural road can lead to such enormous abuse and suffering ...

PROLOGUE

They think they know everything,
but all they know is the news.

– Richard Beard, *Lazarus is Dead*

Breaking news

This is ANA in Luanda, Gaborone, Algiers, Bujumbura and across Africa on TV, on radio and online.

News anchor: Welcome back.
In the run-up to local elections in South Africa next year, one independent candidate has already captured the spotlight. A doctor by profession, Leila Mashal has announced her intention to give up medicine and take up politics. Our reporter John Smith is outside the Great Hall at the University of the Witwatersrand in Johannesburg, where Dr Mashal is about to address a packed auditorium.

Not an obvious choice of venue, John. Is this the start of an elitist campaign for highbrow academics?

Reporter: On the contrary. We've been filming outside the Great Hall here at Wits since the middle of the afternoon, when people started arriving by the busload ahead of the presentation by Dr Mashal, or Leila, as she is more commonly called, and I can tell you, the scenes here have been phenomenal.

Yes, there will of course be academic and specialist interest in what Leila has to say here tonight on a campus where she herself was a student back in the eighties. But remember, universities are not only about the academics and professors you mentioned – more importantly, they are about young people, who are by far the majority on any university campus up and down the country. During the course of the afternoon I've also spoken to many of those in the crowd and, yes, there are trade union representatives and activists and people from the media as one would expect, but there are also civil servants and teachers and health workers and factory workers, refugees, migrants, people from all walks of life, and of course, most strikingly, the young people, the students themselves.

News anchor: In an earlier report, you indicated that organisers had been caught a little off guard and that last-minute contingency plans have had to be made to cater for the crowd. How's that been coming along?

Reporter: Yes, it quickly became clear that, as you say, organisers had underestimated the interest there would be in Dr Mashal's appearance. By late afternoon, extra marshals had to be brought in to help control the enormous crowd that had gathered. We've been told that with the exception of only a very few reserved seats for the most senior university dignitaries, for the rest, those who arrive first are seated first. In fact, the Great Hall here behind me is now full and the doors have already been closed, but if I get our cameraman to pan over the crowd here outside the hall, people who haven't been able to get seats inside, you can see that there are still several hundreds of people here. And this is the reason for the delay in getting things started here tonight. As you can see over there, the organisers have had giant screens set up to relay Dr

Mashal's address from inside the hall to this large overflow crowd here outside.

News anchor: Extraordinary ... Now, I'd like to consider for a moment, if you will, John, the young people you mentioned. How would you explain their interest in an independent candidate so early on in an election campaign? After all, Leila Mashal isn't from a political dynasty, and as an independent she doesn't have the backing or support of huge party machinery.

Reporter: Absolutely. Regarding the younger demographic here tonight, two things. The first: online social networking. You'll remember that Leila Mashal first announced her intention to stand for election on several social networking sites, which we've been told were set up specifically for campaigning reasons.

But, as you also know, while Leila Mashal comes from outside the political establishment, she is not an entirely unknown entity either. She is, of course, also the wife of captured photojournalist Tariq Hassan, whose abduction from a hotel right here in Johannesburg seven months ago made headlines around the world. Up until the abduction, as you've said, she had lived the relatively quiet life of a doctor, working at the Charlotte Maxeke Johannesburg Academic Hospital just up the road from here. And that's where the story turned, and here our viewers will remember the dramatic footage of the abduction filmed on cellphones by people at the scene, footage that of course went viral and has been circulating on the Internet ever since.

So the launch of the Mashal campaign here tonight isn't taking place in a vacuum. On the contrary, the backstory here is enormous. It's not just the high-profile and very public abduction and all the media which that generated, there's also, of course, the ongoing campaign to find Tariq Hassan, and the tens of thousands of young Internet-savvy activists and supporters who have really provided so much of the momentum to this story. You spoke about party machinery earlier. I can tell you, 'party machinery' is perhaps beginning to look somewhat outdated set beside the technological expertise driving the Mashal campaign.

News anchor: And what about her campaign issues, or rather, her campaign issue – because if we've understood correctly, she has only one. Is that right?

Reporter: Quite so, and this is very much the third reason for the diversity of the crowd here tonight. As you've indicated, Mashal is running a single-issue campaign, which isn't about any of the popular or safe electioneering tickets like education or health or employment; it is in fact about something more fundamental than that – freedom. Now, one would have thought that following 1994, voters would see this as a done deal, a battle fought and won, so to speak, but apparently not, if tonight's crowd is anything to go by. For everybody here tonight, that word 'freedom' obviously still resounds.

News anchor: Indeed, it has been two decades since South Africa's transition to democracy and freedom. How would you account for this seemingly anachronistic election issue?

Reporter: Well, we'll have to wait and see how she unravels that here tonight, but I think that if we look at the background to this campaign, implicit is obviously the freedom of her husband, though that – to her credit – has not been exploited by Leila Mashal herself, at least not so far. Whether she'll ratchet that up as her campaign progresses remains to be seen. Another key factor, of course, would be voter disillusionment with the political process, the hubris of the political elite and the corruption. But there's also another, more subtle dimension at play, and here it's worth mentioning the large number of refugees and migrants present here tonight, most of whom won't be able to vote for Leila but have nevertheless still come out to demonstrate their support.

News anchor: In other words, foreign nationals not eligible to vote in South Africa?

Reporter: That's correct. Particularly African foreign nationals. I think this points to the kinds of issues Leila will be addressing tonight when she extrapolates on the issue of freedom. I expect that key amongst her concerns will be issues like safety and security, which Africans have struggled with for decades.

News anchor: Now we're beginning to see images from inside the Great Hall, with the chancellor of the university taking to the stage to introduce Dr Mashal. I wonder if you could tell us quickly, John, what about Leila herself? How does she come across? What can our viewers expect to see tonight?

Reporter: Well, again, we'll have to wait and see,

because other than her brief endorsement of the campaign to find her husband, she really hasn't spoken publicly on very many occasions. Her silence was, of course, a source of frustration for campaigners and activists, at one stage even fuelling speculation as to whether her silence was an indication of complicity in the abduction.

But commentators who have had access to Leila Mashal all seem to be struck by her incredible calm, her quietness and, as somebody said earlier, her eloquence. These are words one hears again and again in relation to her. Whatever it is, she has something, which no doubt all candidates in this election will be watching. But what I will say is this: Whatever that 'something' is, Leila Mashal is due to speak again in Cape Town tomorrow night and Durban on Wednesday. If tonight's crowd here in Johannesburg is anything to go by, my advice to people in those cities who are keen to hear her speak would be to join the queue early.

News anchor: Well, John, thank you for that. We're beginning to hear applause from inside the auditorium now as Leila Mashal makes her way to the podium. She has obviously bided her time and used her silence well till now. Let's cross live now into the auditorium to hear what she has to say.

Somewhere

From beginnings to nursery rhymes ... How the mind leaps from here to there, seeking constant diversion, eternal distraction. I'm lying here again looking at my toes, and perhaps because there are ten of them, and perhaps because they're outlined so clearly against a blank white wall, it's not long before I'm thinking, 'Ten green bottles, hanging from a wall'. But because they're not bottles, they're toes, and because they're not green but brown, my restless mind starts adapting the rhyme, 'Ten brown toes, hanging on a wall, and if one brown toe should accidently fall ...', my mind beginning to envisage the kind of grim circumstances that would lead my toes to be hanging from a wall, being eliminated one by one until eventually none of them remain ...

I must stop this macabre imagining from unfolding further. I take solace that, for now, ten healthy intact toes sprout like muted fingers at the end of two rather enormous feet, the size of which struck me again the other day – which day was that? – when I noticed my heels overhanging the plastic flip-flops with the number 12 stamped into a circle on the underside of their soles. There ... see ... some more distraction, demonstrating again the flitting nature of the mind; toes are simply not compelling enough to keep it focused. Even as I lie here staring at them, it is my feet and the plastic flip-flops that merit description, for what more can be said of toes, what more be thought of them? Unless their nails are being trimmed, and then it's the nails we attend to, unless they're stubbed against the bedpost in the midst of a rush, and then it's the pain we register, what can be more inconsequential in the larger scheme of things than toes? Yet, here I am, once more staring across my reclined body, fingers interlocked behind my head, watching them twitch all of their own accord as even they try to pass the time. And here we go again … another deviation taking shape: no longer bottles, I see these toes of mine mutate into little piggies at the end of my outsized feet. I see the big one getting dressed to go to market, donning a bonnet on its head, swinging a basket by its hand. I see the lazy piggy opting to stay at home, curled up on the sofa to watch omnibus editions of the week's soap operas on daytime TV. A third piggy – this one not so little – sits down at a laden table, tucking a serviette into his collar and licking his lips in expectation of a feast of roast beef.

'It's bacon tomorrow,' I whisper down to him, but all he does is put his podgy little hands on his fat little hips, wiggle them about and mock me.

'Jealousy makes you nasty,' he teases before devouring the cow he'd ambushed after she'd exhausted herself by jumping over the moon. While fat little piggy enjoys his feast, a cruel and unequal world continues to turn, the haves blatantly gorging themselves to excess and in full view of the have-nots. Beside him, a thin, emaciated little piggy sits forlorn with absolutely nothing on his plate, looking as pitiful as Old Mother Hubbard's dog, until eventually even his empty dish abandons him, running away with his spoon. And then I see the fifth little piggy, and how I envy him because he is the one who manages to run right out of this hideous fucking nightmare and all the way home.

You're listening to Global Radio Online. In a change to our regular schedule, next we'll be crossing over live to South Africa, where Dr Leila Mashal, the wife of captured photojournalist Tariq Hassan, is about to make her first public statement since her husband's abduction last year. Dr Mashal will be speaking at Wits University in Johannesburg ...

ANA: Breaking news

Thank you.

When I was a student at this university, I was anxious about having to present my thesis to the panel of experts who would examine me, and worried about not knowing the answers to all the questions they might ask. My supervisor's advice was simple: 'State what you know simply and sincerely. Nobody expects you to know everything. If you don't know an answer, state that simply too. Communicate that the question has opened a door, and demonstrate how you might use your skills to find a responsible answer. And don't elevate the experts too much. Remember that they were once students too.'

I am mindful of her advice as I speak to you here at my old school tonight. It feels good to be back after all these years, this time with a very different kind of thesis. Before I lay it out, let me say that I don't have all the answers, so if you're moved by what I have to say and would like to help, perhaps you might consider joining my small team of volunteers. Before I start, I'd like to thank them.

I have not come here tonight with a long list of promises, few of which I would be able to honour, most of which I would almost certainly not.

I don't have a slick manifesto, written by a team of highly paid consultants in such bland and neutral language as to mean almost anything in almost any context.

I am not here as the candidate of a large political party, which makes decisions high up and far away from the people most affected by them.

I am not here to denigrate the other candidates in this electoral contest.

I am not here tonight to ask for your vote or persuade you of my suitability or assure you of my victory.

These are not my starting points.

I am Leila Mashal and I am here to start a conversation about what I feel to be the most serious threat to our constitutional democracy – such as it is. I am taking the opportunity presented by these elections to start the conversation. I have come to put what I have learned on the agenda for your consideration as you ponder where to place your vote.

I have just one issue for us to consider. You might find it peculiar, my single topic. There are many who would have us view it as 'accomplished'. I believed them too. But that was until seven months ago.

There are many who are surprised at my decision to seek public office, when I seem to be best known as a 'quiet wife'. So am I. Seven months ago I would not have envisaged giving up a career I love – the only job I have ever wanted to do – and certainly not for politics. I would not have foreseen standing here as an independent candidate seeking political office, against a party I have always supported.

But seven months ago, as you already know, I was at one end of a lobby in a Johannesburg hotel while at the other end of that same lobby my husband, Tariq Hassan, was being abducted. In the immediate aftermath of the abduction, the point of impact was personal and therefore private. But during the intervening months, it has become apparent that powerful clandestine and democratically unaccountable forces were involved, which, to my mind, in a transparent and accountable democracy, now makes the issue public.

Since 1994, free and fair elections have apparently become the means by which we determine our political process and the running of this country. But are real power and decision-making necessarily in the hands of the officials we elect? These last seven months I have come to realise that while South Africans hold the vote, they don't hold the power. Our constitutional structures are being hollowed out, withholding power from the electorate and their elected officials and concentrating it in the grip of a secret and unaccountable cabal of oligarchs whose names and faces the electorate will never know. They have a secret ballot all of their own, which is called in a sphere galaxies removed from the reach of the ordinary voter.

Before I even speak the word that was our rallying cry for decades, let us note how unremarkable it has become. How cheap and hollowed-out by spin and slogans. How we have been force-fed the illusion of it by the deeply powerful, to the point of intoxication and trance so that it no longer strikes a chord.

But when the shock wave that took Tariq had retreated, leaving me standing with the realisation that my life had been levelled, that word struck me again – *freedom* – because 'freedom' always comes first.

'Freedom' receives priority treatment in our most binding documents. Article 1 of the Bill of Rights and the Universal Declaration of Human Rights both enshrine freedom first.

And for whom?

In the prior, 'All South Africans are born free and equal'. All South Africans, not only the wealthy.

And in the latter, 'All human beings are born free and equal'. All human beings, not only the powerful.

Freedom first.

For all.

But documents don't ensure in reality the ideas they enshrine in theory. Because even as 'freedom' stands there on paper, foremost amongst the issues we hold most dear, is 'freedom' ever 'done', ever 'achieved', ever 'accomplished'? In South Africa, while 'freedom' was a battle fought, has it ever really been a victory won? How free do you feel?

The operation was swift. Within a matter of minutes, Tariq was gone before most people in the room even knew what had happened. By the following morning, CCTV footage from the hotel surveillance system had vanished, so that the only records of the event are the blurred and shaky images filmed on cellphones and the conflicting statements of 'witnesses' at the scene, all of whom have since disappeared, none of whom the police have been able to trace for clarification or corroboration.

In the seven months since Tariq's abduction, despite

a high-profile police investigation and an ongoing media campaign launched fearlessly and selflessly and tirelessly by his colleagues and associates both here in South Africa and around the world, nobody has come any closer to determining either where Tariq is or what has happened to him. During these seven months, I have cooperated fully with the official police investigation, refraining from speculation in public, declining media interviews, withholding any comments that might either compromise the investigation or aggravate Tariq's position. With the exception of endorsing the campaign spearheaded by his colleagues and associates, my silence has, as advised, been total.

*

On the morning after Tariq's abduction, I did not feel free. During the seven months of his captivity, I have not felt free. I have started to wonder whether I ever was free or whether I ever will be. That is an astonishing reversal because, since 1994, I have gone to bed assuming – if I ever even thought about it – that we had arrived at that place called 'freedom'. On the morning after Tariq's abduction, I woke to the realisation that 'freedom' is not a destination at which one arrives to put up one's feet. 'Freedom' is a journey, a very particular kind of journey. It isn't a drive in a luxury car or a flight on a private jet. It isn't a big house in a plush suburb. It isn't private schools and shopping malls. It is an ongoing pursuit, an endeavour, a long and difficult walk.

So what am I to do now? Carry on the zombie talk and walk of the 'peaceful transition' when in fact there has been no transition at all, least of all a peaceful one?

Continue to wave flags for the myth of the 'rainbow nation' when in reality we live in the most unequal country on earth, but actually I'm quite well off, thank you very much, so why should I care?

They say that the longest journey starts with the first step, so let me take that first step now, in front of you, and in so doing let me be clear: what happened to Tariq could happen to anybody. There are forces of deep power now at work in this country, manipulating its institutions, its systems and its structures. We are not ruled by a government. We are overseen by a cabal of deeply powerful conglomerates and our elected leaders are merely their enforcers. What happened to Tariq arose out of that cabal, with its tentacles tightly wound around every aspect of life in this country, including and especially our political processes. That invisible cabal of deep power has no truck with constitutions or manifestos or binding documents enshrining civil rights and liberties. Its only concern is the protection of its own interests, whatever the cost. Such indiscriminate power does not affect Tariq alone. It also affects you.

And so, in reality, this is not an issue only about Tariq, and I am very aware that his fate has made the news. That is something. And if he is never found …

And if he is never found, it will be a long time before he is forgotten. That is something too. But the shameful plight of most South Africans happens off the radar and far away from the cameras. They are the anonymous and the nameless, whose suffering we have come to hold in contempt and whose grinding poverty and insecurity we dismiss when it does make the news. The humiliation they suffered during the apartheid era, under a government they did not elect, is the same humiliation they suffer in the post-apartheid era, under a government they did. That makes it an especially bitter pill to swallow.

This is not only a story about Tariq. The default response of the 'legacy of apartheid' to explain away the suffering of most South Africans when this country's largest post-apartheid expenditure has been not on housing, or education, or health, or development, or any of those safe electioneering issues you will soon hear bandied about, but on the illegal and corrupt purchase of weapons – which conservative estimates place at R30 billion within the first five years of the post-apartheid era. Then came the 2010 FIFA World Cup – from which street vendors were kept away by 'exclusion zones' and the homeless banished to 'temporary relocation areas' – now estimated to have cost more than R27 billion. That's at least R57 billion not spent on housing or education or health, but on guns and football. When did we forget that 'people are the real wealth of a nation', not markets or minerals or investor confidence? No, this is not a story only about Tariq. To make it so would be diminishment. It is a story about everybody, including you.

Let me tell you why.

In the months since the abduction, I have complied fully with the advice given to me by those conducting the official police investigation, which was to maintain public silence. I have, however, written privately and personally to the local member of parliament deployed to my area, to my premier, to the commissioner of police, to the minister of home affairs and to the presidency with information which suggests that:

- the abduction was meticulously planned;
- it was specifically planned inside the Republic;

- it was executed by professionals;
- crucial evidence was 'lost';
- key 'witnesses' were staged;
- in the absence of a ransom request, this was not a kidnapping for quick financial gain;
- the level of expertise involved would have been expensive;
- given Tariq's total disappearance, in all probability to somewhere outside of the Republic, his abduction will have entailed third-party knowledge, involvement and support, probably at the level of state or states; and
- excluding agents of the state, in South Africa only a relatively small number of specially trained private military operatives would have the ability, resources and expertise to execute such a complex abduction so efficiently, thereby narrowing down considerably the list of potential perpetrators.

Do you feel free? How free should I feel?

As we approach this election, consider this. In South Africa today, the state no longer has exclusive rights to the use of force against its citizens. In fact, force has also become the prerogative of giant national and multinational corporations of privatised military and security expertise, which now exceeds that of the state by five to one. According to the Minister of Safety and Security, Charles Nqakula, 'The entire complement of people who are under arms in the private security industry is larger than the number of people in the armed forces.'

How free do you feel?

Consider that in South Africa today, for each state agent there are five private agents whose access to force is outside the control of the state. Neither you nor the democratic systems of the state – such as they are – govern those five agents. Instead, while they have the capacity to deploy levels of force that surpass those of the state, they have no democratic accountability to you or the state. While state agents are accountable, should be accountable, to you, the electorate, private agents are accountable only to shareholders, shareholders for whom force is profit.

But why should this matter? Because if you are poor and faced with a daily barrage of urban violence and crime, what comfort do you take in the fact that your government, having transformed state responsibilities into market opportunities from which only a small elite profits, has privatised nearly every basic state responsibility, including its responsibility to protect you? Instead, if you are poor in South Africa today, you can't expect to feel free, because you can't afford to pay for the privilege.

And if you are wealthy, how free should you feel knowing that this private protection, which you have acquired by virtue of your resources, is not accountable to you? Private force is accountable only to private profit.

*

Such an arsenal of private force has the capacity to undermine and threaten the democratic procedures of the state. I say 'democratic procedures' because in transparent and accountable democracies, force should be public, the state strictly sanctioned in its use. I say 'democratic procedures' because in democracies, elected officials should be the guardians of force. Instead, in South Africa today, elected officials are the enforcers of multinational conglomerates whose neocolonial agenda for a new world order controls all the major institutions of this country. I say 'democratic procedures' because in democracies, agents of force should be accountable and constitutionally governed, the various arms of the state governing deployment, the state ultimately governed by you, the electorate. I say 'ultimately governed by you' because rich or poor, the deployment of force ultimately affects you because deployment ultimately affects your freedom.

In South Africa, where force should be under the scrutiny of civilian leadership, it is instead civilians who are increasingly under the scrutiny of private, unaccountable and unconstitutional force. When did this silent inversion in the balance of surveillance take place? Was it while I was in the cinema? Was it while I was visiting the National Arts Festival in Grahamstown? Was it when I was out shopping in the mall? Was it while I was on a family vacation in Plettenberg Bay? Was it when I was in a restaurant sharing a meal with friends? Was it that weekend I went to Oppikoppi? At which point in my life as a 'free' citizen did the balance of power over me shift from the people I elected to unaccountable forces whose faces I don't know? Was it while we were out celebrating our freedom when really all we had been given was the illusion thereof?

When Tariq was abducted, I received messages of support from diplomats and ambassadors, celebrities and civilians, poets and preachers from around the world, but from my elected officials, nothing. The questions I ask are: Why the silence? Why my silence? Why the silence of my elected officials? In 1970 Ruth First wrote that 'power lies in the hands of those who control the means of violence'. Who controls the means of violence in South Africa today?

These past seven months have led me to the following conclusion. In truth, when it comes to profit, our government is no nobler than governments the world over who have been left paralysed by the power of profit and held to ransom by the profit of privatisation. In the last decade, South Africans have witnessed the privatisation, or the attempt at privatisation, the marketeering, of nearly every primary state responsibility, including water, electricity, health care, housing, transport, communications and arms, the buying and selling of their core concerns. What we are beginning to witness in South Africa today are the workings of the deep force behind the 'elected' force, the deep power behind the 'elected' power. In the seven months since Tariq's abduction, it has become clear that his capture was at the hands of that deep force now so woven into the fabric of our system as to have access to the highest offices in the land, where it can place unelected fingers on elected lips and ensure they remain silent.

My detractors argue that I have no chance of winning

a safe municipal ward. Perhaps. But at this early stage, it's not about winning. It's about starting the conversation. My elected officials would not heed my correspondence. Perhaps they'll listen to me now.

And so I wish to send a clear message to my government tonight. While it deals in silence, I do not. While it has been silenced, I have not. Instead, I will apply all my energy and resources towards injecting this issue into the public domain and onto the political agenda because South Africa is being held ransom by covert undemocratic and unelected forces.

Freedom?

Tariq is not free.

I am not free.

There is no freedom.

There is only the fight for freedom.

Relay: Atouf/Johannesburg

In Palestine, this is the worst of times – everywhere, the same reality. In the village of Tammoun, Diab Bsharat, an English teacher and father of five, is one of 160 000 unpaid civil servants across the country. In addition to his own children, he is also responsible for his younger brother Ayman's education, but is unable to meet the cost. A civil engineering student, Ayman would have registered for his final year at university in September.

'Now I cannot,' Ayman says. 'I have only one year left to complete my degree, but I cannot. These sanctions don't punish Hamas. They punish all the Palestinian people.'

Ayman has words. In the village clinic, the lab technician has only tears. She works onerous shifts on antiquated equipment with no pay. When I ask about her children, she weeps ...

SOMEWHERE

I'm trying to keep track, trying to follow the trail of breadcrumbs from colourful rhymes to washed-out circles of grey. The fifth little piggy has made it home, but I remain stuck and the nightmare continues. I try desperately to think of something new, something never before thought, but everything has stopped. No new input, just recycled repetition running on a loop. Nobody has told me anything. No rubbing together, no collisions, none of that stimulating friction, no brushing into the lives of others, no new sparks to ignite my atrophying mind. I have not read anything or heard anything other than that constant low background drone. I have not touched anything but these four walls and this hard mattress for … for I really don't know how long. Measured time has stopped. Zombie time marches on. All I have is memories, rehearsed for all this time and endlessly repeated, so washed out and threadbare they're beginning to soak into one another, like colours seeping in the wash, the life of my mind circling in on itself, round and round and round until eventually everything comes out the same dull grey.

News anchor: And rapturous applause there for Leila Mashal speaking at Wits. With me here in the studio listening to her are Professor Muriel Hastings from the Department of Political Science at the University of Cape Town, and Dr Teboho Mofokeng from the Institute for Security Studies in Pretoria. Professor Hastings, let's start with you ...

Editorial

~Leila Mashal~
Morning Herald, 5 February 20—

Let's start with the applause inside the hall. Two things were striking. It was deafening. And it was sustained. The question is why? The answer is simple. Because in her first public address since the abduction of her husband, Tariq Hassan, delivered at the University of the Witwatersrand last night, Leila Mashal spoke the truth and she spoke it plainly. In a political wilderness of repetitive bland rhetoric in which all politicians have come to sound like all other politicians, here was a new, brave voice. What's more, in a political wilderness of dull, shrill and uninspiring independent candidates, here finally is a new vibrant force. If Leila Mashal wins, there will be no stopping her and those who were present in the Great Hall at Wits last night will have witnessed a turning point in our political path. Our elected officials, if they were not listening, should have been. Dr Mashal has drawn a line in the sand. Are they brave enough to cross it? Last night Leila Mashal reminded us of one word – freedom. This morning we shout three: 'Go, Leila, go!'

PART I

Don't shoot what it looks like.
Shoot what it feels like.

– David Alan Harvey, photographer

Two images

Two images accompanied the announcement of Tariq Hassan's abduction: one, the award-winning photograph he had taken eighteen months earlier, which had come to epitomise the horror of the civil war in Kasalia; the other, amateur footage of his elegant wife, standing alone in the hotel foyer from where he had been seized, absent-mindedly fingering the diamond pendant around her neck.

The photograph is deceptive – a girl and a man, silhouetted against a red desert background, hovering above a mirage – at first sight, the kind of idealised depiction of rural privation so indulgently romanticised in banal watercolours and sentimental greeting cards. But in this deception lay its command; it seems to be one thing while really it is something else completely, its apparently facile surface lowering your guard, drawing you in, before its gruesome details devour your neutered assumptions and spit them out: the girl, scantily clad, leading the man through a scorched, blistering wasteland, the lap of her torn dress stained red, rivulets of coagulated blood encrusted down the inside of her legs, the man's swollen lids pierced through with thorns.

'An ambush in a frame,' one reviewer had called it.

'Hassan's extraordinary photograph usurps all the mind-numbing techniques of blinkered portraiture, flipping expressions like no other contemporary depiction. I have seen women cross their legs as the realisation of what had befallen the girl dawns.'

Eighteen months after it first dominated the front pages, the photograph was once again in the headlines, the backdrop against which newsreaders announced the abduction of the man who made it, renowned journalist and writer Tariq Hassan. Hastily culled photographs of Hassan himself were not broadcast until several hours later. His own face eclipsed, he had become completely identifiable by his work. Circumstances aside, for a maker of pictures who himself preferred to remain invisible, that at least would surely have pleased him.

Less comforting would have been the amateur footage of a speeding car, a confused crowd and his lost wife, captured on a mobile phone by a bystander at the scene.

'We don't really know what happened,' the young Kasalian man commented on his footage.

'I had come to hear him speak. I admire his work. He brought the war in my country to the world's attention. With one photograph he did more to stop it than the UN did with a hundred toothless resolutions. I wanted to meet him and have my book signed,' he said, holding up his copy.

'The foyer was crowded with people waiting. Then there was a sudden surge at the door. I assumed he had arrived so I turned on my camera. Then I heard screeching tyres. I turned to look. It all happened so fast. I did not imagine that Tariq Hassan was being abducted in that car. If I had, I would have aimed at a clearer shot. But the car was gone before I even located it properly. I turned the camera back over the crowd. As you can see, there was a lot of confusion and people rushing to the door. As the room emptied, I noticed this woman standing by herself at the back of the foyer. To be honest, I just thought she was beautiful, so I filmed her. I got a few seconds of her before the recording timed out. By this time I was starting to piece together what had happened. I didn't know who the woman was, but I remember thinking that in all the confusion, there was something in her quiet expression that captured perfectly the severity of the moment.'

This is the BBC World Service. In South Africa this week Leila Mashal broke her silence, outlining the threat to the state and to constitutional democracy posed by private security firms in South Africa. Her speech has caused political fallout in South Africa and beyond, reigniting the debate here in Britain about plans to privatise the police. Supporters of the move claim that a privatised police force will provide a better, more efficient service to the public while ensuring a safer society. Detractors argue it will compromise state security by creating a private force accountable only to private companies and shareholders. What do you think? Are there similar proposals in your country? Do get in touch. We'd like to hear your views. Our first caller is Zia from Pakistan. Hello, Zia …

'Missing him already?'

The light is fading. I'm sitting at the kitchen table. Tariq's desk chair would be more comfortable, but I still can't go into that room. Tapping the tip of my pencil on the page, I am reminded of a game we used to play as children. It involved picking up sticks, isolating one stick from a tangle of sticks and then removing it carefully without disturbing the pack. The challenge was in choosing the first stick to remove from the tangled mess without causing the fragile world of teetering sticks to collapse.

I'm sitting in the dark. For now that simple statement will have to suffice. It's not a good stick to contemplate. I'm remembering our last holiday together. Perhaps that is a better stick to choose. There was moonlight on coconut palms. We were swaying in a hammock on a long stretch of open beach. The tide was in and the sea was lapping gently just below our dangling feet.

'Do you remember that story I once told you?' Tariq says.

'Which one?' I ask. 'You've told me so many.'

'The one about the Eritrean prisoner in the Ethiopian jail.'

'We're supposed to be on holiday. Try to think pleasant thoughts.'

'Tried.' He shrugged. 'Can't stop remembering.'

I run my fingers through his hair. 'It was a long time ago … Tell me again.'

*

He was a doctor. He and a group of his colleagues had been rounded up from their night shift at the hospital for 'unpatriotic activities' and driven away into the night. I met him a few years after his release. It was my last night in Addis. He'd been in prison for ten years – nobody knew where. Even his family had given up hope. He'd spent most of that time in solitary isolation … Can you imagine? Ten years … Alone …

I asked him how he'd coped.

'*Anna Karenina*,' he said.

I waited for the details, but none came. We sat there for a long while, sipping beer, smoking strong Egyptian cigarettes.

'You had access to books, then?' I probed.

He looked away from me, his eyes eventually settling on something in the distance.

'It was many months into our isolation. I had begun to sense that my compatriot in the next cell was beginning to … unravel? I knew Morse code from my sailing days, so I devised a system to teach him the code. It was complex, but made sense under the circumstances. I'd tap gently on the wall between us whenever it was safe. It took ages, but it was a project. It had meaning. It kept our minds occupied. Once he knew the code, I started tapping him a story.'

'*Anna Karenina*?' I guessed.

'It was the longest story I could think of. I'd read the novel at university. It took years. Looking back, I'm not sure that my code or my version of *Anna Karenina* was accurate. It may have included my own fabrications and special effects. But it got him through. And me.'

*

Outside my captors move from blackened window to blackened window, their torches hacking like machetes at the night. From my position I see their shapes as they press their beams against the windowpanes, trying to establish my whereabouts inside the house.

'Dr Mashal?' they call out.

I ignore them. Do they think I have escaped? I hear them exchange whispers before one of them moves urgently to the front of the house.

'Dr Mashal?'

I imagine what might happen if I continue to ignore them. I suppose they would radio for support before repositioning their armoured vehicle to face the house, glowing and purring like a giant automated creature ready to pounce. Minutes later their reinforcements will arrive: more armoured vehicles, a helicopter hovering overhead. Secure in strength and numbers, they will enter the house wearing night-vision goggles, moving from room to room, rifles at the ready. Of course they'll find me sitting here, in my small corner. Their wild fantasies of my daring escape and their brave chase will crumble, leaving only the anticlimax of superheroes all dressed up but with nowhere to go.

Time moves slowly. Sometimes I bump up against it, like a rear-end collision, when it suddenly grinds to a halt in front of me while my mind has been occupied elsewhere.

Tariq! Where the hell are you? Are you happy now? Come. Take a photo of me now, sitting here, small in my small corner. What will you see, Tariq? Tell me. What will you see?

'Why not come as far as Cairo?' he suggested. 'You've always wanted to. Now's your chance.'

I resisted. In the early days, before the extreme became routine, it used to unsettle me, life with a man whose life was trauma.

'And what happens when you go to Libya?'

'Don't worry. You'll be well taken care of. And I'll be back before you know it.'

I hesitated.

'What's to think about?'

'It's not how I imagined my first trip to Egypt would be.'

'Then stay at home. No destination is ever as you expect it to be.'

A few hours into the flight, dinner had been served and the cabin was quiet. To my left, Tariq had fallen asleep. To my right, a man was reading a newspaper that had been distributed by a flight attendant. I noticed a headline as he turned the page and leaned forward to retrieve my copy from the seat pocket in front of me.

No-Man's-Land for Palestinians with No Land

Cairo
30 September 1995

The Commissioner-General for the United Nations Relief and Works Agency for Palestinian Refugees (UNRWA) and the United Nations High Commissioner for Refugees (UNHCR) have called on the Libyan government to resolve the crisis facing 30 000 stateless Palestinian refugees being expelled from Libya.

Having been denied entry into Egypt, thirty-two Palestinians are currently stranded in the no-man's-land between the borders of Libya and Egypt, including several young children and a five-month-old baby. A further 1 500 people are being evicted to enclosed camps in the desert outside Tobruk, near the Egyptian border.

The refugees have been expelled by Libyan leader Muammar Gaddafi in condemnation of the newly formed Palestinian National Authority and as a rebuke for the Palestinian Liberation Organization's peace with Israel. 'Since the Palestinian leaders claim they have now got a homeland and a passport, let the 30 000 Palestinians in Libya go back to their homeland and let's see if Israel would permit them to return,' the Libyan leader said. 'That's how the world will find out that the peace it's been advocating is no more than treachery and a conspiracy.'

Neighbouring Arab states have all refused entry to the refugees.

A lift delivered us swiftly to the top floor of a plush hotel, generously chosen by my dissident guardian so that I might benefit from the views. Below, a relentless city marched out to defy an even more relentless desert. Yahya, quietly attentive, constantly vigilant, joined me by the window.

'They're switching on the night,' he said as countless flashing neon signs large as cinema screens and green fluorescent lights illuminating a thousand minarets began to flicker across the city.

'Which way is Libya?' I asked.

'There.' Yahya gestured confidently, and I followed the direction of his pointing finger over the pianist's head, through the window, across the Nile and into the desert where the sun was setting. I cursed Tariq for bringing me here, then leaving me for Libya.

'Missing him already?' Yahya asked, stooping to find my eyes.

The truth is, I am always missing Tariq because Tariq is always gone. Gone to Chechnya. Gone to Rwanda. Gone to Afghanistan. Gone to Libya. As soon as it was made, Yahya's observation so subtly disguised as a question – 'Missing him already?' – I knew that Yahya, still a stranger, had pointed at the very core of my being as clearly and as confidently as he had pointed at Libya. There was a beginning, the realisation that I would always be missing Tariq.

Relay: Johannesburg/Kas

Weep. Who still weeps in the European Union? Survey the raised hands. There would be a telling demographic. Vote. Who in Europe bothers? In a country already under military occupation, the issues stack up – refugees, military incursions, territorial dismembering, checkpoints, prisoners, child prisoners, settlements, the Wall, unemployment, poverty, sanctions and now the debilitating battle between Fatah and Hamas. 'The worst of times' is no understatement. War on Want estimates that 60 per cent of Palestinians now face acute poverty, a tripling in four years …

Your Most Precious Things

This is ANA in Kampala, Nairobi, Addis Ababa, Windhoek and across Africa on TV, on radio and online.

Douglas Thompson was reading from Lazarus is Dead *by Richard Beard, abridged for radio by Sue Scott. The producer was Mervin January. In tomorrow's episode, while Lazarus's condition deteriorates, the miracles of his estranged childhood friend grow more spectacular. Lazarus will do anything to restore his health, except take the advice of his desperate sisters – to call for Jesus.*

Looking ahead to eleven o'clock this morning, as the anniversary of South Africa's first democratic elections approaches, our correspondent Neil Jeffries has been travelling around the country meeting young South Africans born on that historic day, 27 April 1994. What do they know about apartheid? What are their experiences growing up in the new South Africa? That's Born Free? *with Neil Jeffries, just after the news headlines at eleven.*

But first, here's Sue Dayton with this week's edition of Your Most Precious Things. *Sue's guest this week is the award-winning photojournalist Tariq Hassan.*

Presenter: Welcome to *Your Most Precious Things*, the show that invites prominent personalities to choose three items they would save from a house fire. As always, the items must be inanimate objects. Human beings and pets will have been saved by rescue services. They must also be objects our guests can carry themselves with relative ease. So I'm sorry to say that as much as you might love the baby grand, it will have to succumb to the flames. If you can't carry it, you can't save it.

My guest this week is, in a very real sense, always in the news or, to be more exact, behind the news, making it, sometimes writing it and, more famously, recording the images that convey it. Most well known for his intimate depictions of people made vulnerable by conflict and war, he recently received the prestigious Platinum Lens Award for journalistic photography in recognition of his work documenting the civil war in Kasalia. He is, of course, the photojournalist Tariq Hassan. Welcome.

Tariq: Thank you.

Presenter: So, the Platinum Lens. That's a big one. Congratulations. It must bring a huge sense of accomplishment having your work acknowledged in this way.

Tariq: It does. And I feel very humbled.

Presenter: Of course our listeners will be most familiar with that now iconic photograph of a father and daughter escaping the civil war in Kasalia. And for those of you who haven't seen the photo yet, it's on our website right now. To quote one of the comments

I've read about that photograph, 'If ever there was an image that captured the horror of the war in Kasalia, Tariq Hassan's is that image.'

The comment is obviously intended as praise for an exceptional image. But another way of putting it would be to say, 'Tariq Hassan photographs horror well'. How would you respond to that?

Tariq: I think I'd say that I photograph life and that sometimes, often, life is horrible. How well I do or don't do that is really for the viewer to decide. People will look at an image and it will either stop them or it won't. They'll decide either 'I like that', in which case they'll stop to have a closer look, or 'I don't like that', in which case they'll move on and not think twice about it.

And I say 'I photograph life' because, regarding the Kasalia image, when I saw those people walking out of that war, I saw life, the sheer will and determination to put one foot in front of the other and to carry on. You know, when I'm back in the city, I hear a million people complain about a million things and, really, it's all bullshit. To them I say, 'Take a moment to stand in that girl's shoes, to take her father by the hand and lead him through a war.' To me, they are an affirmation of courage, of strength, of determination and of the absolute refusal, whatever the odds, to just lie down and die.

Presenter: Newborn babies, kittens and meadows in spring – they're life as well, yet you specifically don't photograph those.

Tariq: No, I don't.

Presenter: Why not?

Tariq: I suppose because they're easy subjects. They require little mediation. They require little protection. Their rights are guaranteed, more or less. People, at least most people, already identify with and feel protective towards those subjects. Kittens and puppies and cute babies, our attitudes towards them are largely positive. They'll be fine. I guess I'm more concerned with contexts in which emotions are more ambiguous, where conventional societal responses are less clearly defined.

Presenter: 'Ambiguous.' That's a good word. I'd like to come back to it later, but before we do that, it's time to tell us about the first object you'd save if your house burnt down.

Tariq: In my studio at home I have some of the old equipment from my father's studio – cameras, tripods, lighting equipment and the rest, even a backdrop of the grand staircase of the Paris opera house. My father used to have one of those old-fashioned photo parlours in Durban where families would come back in the sixties and seventies to have their portraits taken. There's also a box of old family photos, some black and white, some dating back to the fifties, the kind with decorative scalloped edges. I remember my father going through those photographs when I was growing up. He could talk for hours about the lives of the people in those pictures. This isn't something we do so much any more. Digital techniques have done away with the family album as I knew it. Of course I'd like to save all of these things from the fire, but I can't, so I'd have to choose just one object from that era, which would be the first camera I ever owned, a gift from my father. It was an Olympus Trip 35, a regular point-and-shoot, extremely simple to use, probably one of the most popular cameras of all time. But to me it's so much more than that. For me, it represents my father's acknowledgement that I had a talent for pictures, if you like, the moment when I knew that he knew that he and I had the same talent. That Trip represents for me the moment when my father demonstrated that he knew me. I was over the moon.

Presenter: And how old were you at the time?

Tariq: I was eight.

Presenter: So you've always known what you wanted to do with your life, or at least from very early on.

Tariq: Without a doubt.

Presenter: And to what would you attribute that clarity of vision?

Tariq: To my father. I adored him. I wanted to be him. I idolised my father in a way most boys idolise their dads, but it wasn't because he had the fastest car or the biggest house or any of those things. On the contrary, I had a very modest upbringing. It had more to do with the fact that what my father did I saw as magic.

These days, cameras are everywhere and everybody is a drive-by photographer, but back then, when I was growing up, photography was more special. Most people, most homes, didn't have cameras. Going back to the Trip my father gave me, back then it was a big deal. I remember talking about it in class and my teacher asking me to bring it in to show and to give a special presentation on how it worked. Can you imagine? So back then people would dress up in their best clothes and come to my father's studio to have their portraits taken. And that small studio in Durban was where I grew up. Being an only child, my mother having died when I was very young, that studio was where I went after school and at weekends. When I was a boy I would mostly watch from behind the scenes – the special clothes and the make-up and the poses and of course the darkroom, which was my absolute favourite. To me, images appearing on blank paper in water was just amazing.

Plus, of course, the one thing that was crucial to my father's job was that he made people smile. 'Say cheese!' And they did. They always seemed happier when they left with their portraits than when they arrived.

Presenter: Yet it would be fair to say that smiling is perhaps not the most common reaction to your own photography.

Tariq: That would be a fair observation, yes.

Presenter: Why is that?

Tariq: Well, my father took very different photographs from mine. His work took place in a studio, very much a controlled, make-believe environment. My father created idealised portraiture of people, less as they were and more as they wanted to be, portraits in make-believe settings ...

Presenter: Like the Paris opera house.

Tariq: Exactly, like the Paris opera house. And as with the opera house, so with the smile – it was very important to smile, to project a carefree image even though it might not be entirely genuine. If people believed ... or rather, if people were willing to suspend disbelief about the authenticity of the Paris opera house, why not also about the sincerity of the smile?

Presenter: Pastiche.

Tariq: And veneer. Surface. Whereas the kinds of images I try to capture are less controlled. For a start, they don't ever happen in studios and I never tell my subjects to 'smile'.

Presenter: It's lovely to hear you speak, but the world is burning. Time to save your second object from the fire.

Tariq: It would be a photograph that was taken in Afghanistan in 2004 by a long-time associate and friend of mine. He was born in Kabul, but his family, like so many Afghan families, had fled the country following the Soviet invasion in 1979. This was his first trip back in nearly twenty-five years. He was taking his children, all of whom had been born in exile in Switzerland, to visit their ancestral home near Kabul. As it happened, I was in Peshawar at the time and accepted an invitation to join him and his family for part of their trip.

On our last afternoon in Afghanistan, my friend drove us to an open-air theatre in Kabul, a place where families would go when he was a child to picnic and to watch films or listen to live music concerts. My friend had been quite excited at the prospect of returning all those years later to a place filled with special childhood memories, but this being Afghanistan, which is easily the most war-ravaged country on earth, he was also apprehensive about what he might find.

I can still see his face, the expression on his face, change as he got out of the car, eyes closed, full of hope that perhaps this one place from his childhood might miraculously have been spared the destruction that had been meted out everywhere else, only to realise, eyes opened, that, like everywhere else, it too had been devastated by war. Nothing of the Afghanistan he knew and remembered remained intact. Everything had been destroyed. Thankfully, you and I don't know what that must feel like, to see everything you have ever known about home, all your memories, lie in ruins. That is a peculiarly Afghan experience, your whole world literally burned down. We are indulging in hypothesis here, hypothetical infernos, but for many people in Afghanistan, having to save their world from flames is a real experience. I'll never forget my friend's expression as he surveyed those ruins. If ever a man aged a hundred years in a moment, then that was it …

I can still see his face at that moment as clearly as I can see this microphone in front of me. It was one of those moments that … I don't know … This might sound strange coming from a photographer, but some moments are just too sacred to be photographed. And in those moments, all you can do, all you should do, is acknowledge them, live fully in them, then let them pass. My friend's moment of realisation has passed and I was privileged to be there to witness it with him. But if I ever take up painting one day, it would be to paint only one portrait – of my friend's face at that moment of truth. I think, or at least I'd like to think, that if such a portrait were ever to be painted and if it were to be any good, then all those who have ever known the destruction of war would recognise and identify with the expression on the face of such a portrait.

Later that afternoon, my friend snatched up my camera to photograph his young daughters skipping around on the stage of the ruined theatre. He wasn't a photographer but, in a single shot, he took the perfect picture. By now the sun was setting behind the theatre. In the background are the bullet-ridden walls around the stage. With the sun streaming in from behind, the effect is similar to that of sunlight filtering through thick lace curtains. In the foreground are the silhouettes of his young daughters skipping on the stage, arms outstretched like poised dancers, their scarves and skirts suspended in the wind.

It was a single shot confidently taken, without hesitation or deliberation. He just reached for the camera, aimed and clicked. I was facing away from the stage, but it happened so quickly that by the time I turned around to see what he was photographing, the girls had left the stage and were running back towards us. And then he handed the camera back to me, switching it off as he did so. I remember that very clearly, how he very specifically and knowingly switched off the camera as he handed it back, all the time maintaining full eye contact. Once I'd taken hold of the camera, he nodded, patted me firmly on the shoulder, and led us back to the car without once looking back. Sometimes …

Sometimes fact …

Sometimes fact really is stranger than fiction ... My friend never saw the photograph he had taken. He died that night, in his sleep, in his ancestral home, on his last night in Afghanistan. They had been due to fly back to Switzerland the following day. When the physician asked his wife how she would explain his sudden death, she spoke two words: 'Shattered memories.'

Presenter: You're listening to *Your Most Precious Things*, with special guest Tariq Hassan.

I'm interested to hear you say that some moments are just too sacred to be photographed. You've just shared a very intimate story, and your own photography too is typified by extremely intimate depictions of people in extremely vulnerable circumstances. Do you think photography can be intrusive? Do you ever feel as though you are intruding on personal tragedies?

Tariq: Abusive photography is intrusive, by which I mean the kind of photography taken by photographers who hound their subjects and violate their privacy and are generally unwelcome at the scene. In my experience there is always a subtle contract, or perhaps 'agreement' would be a better word, a subtle agreement between a photographer and his subject, a fine balance. Kind of like a waltz of consent, if you like, in which one party agrees to make revelations which the other party will record. The best photographs happen – to my mind the best images are recorded – when the relationship is consensual. An ethical photographer is always aware of this delicate balance and never disturbs it. The lens is not dissimilar to the eye. We all know when it's prudent to look away. It's instinctive. That is the first thing. The second thing has to do with the relationship you set up with your subject. I have never felt as though I was intruding on personal tragedies because none of my intimate subjects have been complete strangers to me.

Presenter: So have you known all the people you have photographed?

Tariq: Your surprise suggests an assumption that one would arrive at a scene and immediately start photographing. Of course that is what some photographers do and that is up to them. But I couldn't do that. I prefer to spend time with my subjects before I ever reach for my camera, to speak to them, to get to know their stories, their worries, their concerns. I think that's how one sets up intimacy and elicits the approval of your subjects so that they know that you are sincerely interested in them and in telling their story.

Presenter: You're right. I am surprised and I did assume. So if we take the Kasalian images, for example: did you know the girl and her father?

Tariq: I did indeed. I'd been in Kasalia for six months, travelling around different regions of the country trying to capture the nuances of a very complex and multifaceted war with many different players, some known, others more covert. By the time I took that photograph, I'd been living in their village for three weeks. It's in the heart of a particularly brutal theatre of the war. I was there on the night the village was sacked. I took that photograph the following day, when we were walking to the UN camp for IDPs.

Presenter: Internally displaced persons.

Tariq: That's correct.

Presenter: Now you've described this part of the country as being a particularly brutal theatre of the war. Why is that?

Tariq: As I've already said, the civil war in Kasalia is an enormously complex battle ground of internal and external and government and rebel and covert forces, but what's important to know is that it all comes down to the control of mineral resources, especially tantalum, a metal used in the manufacture of electronic devices – cellphones, DVD players, and so forth. If you control access and production and distribution, well, you're sitting on a gold mine.

Presenter: Or a tantalum mine, as the case may be.

Tariq: Absolutely.

Presenter: So just talk us through the dynamics a little bit more. You're in this village. I think it's called Degongu; is that right?

Tariq: Yes, Degongu.

Presenter: So you're in Degongu, in the worst affected region of a protracted and bloody civil war. I mean, some of the details are just chilling. I'm reminded of another review of your photograph: 'I have seen women cross their legs as the realisation of what had befallen the girl dawns.' Obviously gruesome stuff.

Why such brutality in Degongu?

Tariq: There are as many possible answers to that question as there are victims in this conflict. And it depends on whom you speak to and whom that person is speaking for. But in many ways this war mirrors other wars like it. Countries that have a history of civil war are more likely to have civil wars, as are countries with hostile neighbours, countries with weak or no central government, poor countries, ethnically diverse countries, mineral-rich countries, landlocked countries, even mountainous ... Did you know that civil wars are more likely to occur in mountainous countries than in flat ones? Kasalia has all these features. Parts of the country, particularly the region of Degongu, are outside the control of central government, leaving a security vacuum in which factionalism and impunity thrive. Plus there is the ready availability of arms and guns for hire and virtually little or no legal framework, regulation or system of accountability. It's very much the kind of world in which, as someone once said, 'You're guilty until proven rich'. So people get killed. How brutally depends on the whim of the killer.

But there's also something to say here about our basest instincts and some of our oldest stories. As in so many conflicts, the base instinct in Kasalia is not Kasalian greed but human greed, and it's important to remember that conflict zones are quite 'cosmopolitan' places, in that they attract people from all over the world, whether to fight, or fuel, or profit, or help, or protest, or record. However much we might deny it, we all have a vested interest, whether we're aware of it or not. In the case of Kasalia, where the vested interest is tantalum, the mineral's name itself is especially interesting because it derives from Tantalus, the son of Zeus, who offended the gods by serving the dismembered remains of his son at a banquet. As punishment, Tantalus was banished to the underworld, where food and water remain just beyond his reach, leaving his basic needs unquenched – hence the verb 'to tantalise'. So Tantalus is condemned to a constant state of yearning for what is unobtainable.

Presenter: That's fascinating ...

You spoke earlier about emotionally ambiguous contexts. I'd like to explore this notion of ambiguity a bit more, especially moral ambiguity when it comes to the role of the photographer in conflict situations. Often one hears debates about the moral and ethical responsibility photographers have towards their subjects and whether photographers should intervene to prevent the horror they're recording – in other words, put down the camera and help. What are your thoughts on this? Do you ever feel conflicted?

Tariq: I have to say I instinctively bristle against the question because it's an old one and in my experience it most often gets asked by people who don't do anything to help anyway, armchair observers and remote-control jockeys. But setting that aside, I would ask another set of questions. In most of the contexts I have worked in, photographers and journalists and aid workers are frequently the only outsiders at the scene. So it's very seldom an either-or situation anyway. In fact, while war is chaos, a fair amount of it is also organisation, and there is a lot of collaboration between journalists and aid workers in conflict zones and emergency-response situations because aid workers realise that they also have a responsibility to tell the story. One of my issues is this: if there is a crisis, what skills can you bring to that situation? Clearly, I am not a doctor and I cannot bring that set of skills to an emergency. But let's say that somebody was dying and I was the only person present. I've already spoken about sacred moments, and if the choice was holding a dying man's hand or holding a camera, I know what I would do.

Another scenario, for example, is the real case of ... the real case of ... I'm sorry. I was going to say one thing but found myself recalling another. Your listeners might remember that iconic photograph of the Buddhist monk Thich Quang Duc who set himself alight in protest against the US-backed government of South Vietnam. It's a remarkable photograph and also a very chilling image. It forced President Kennedy to change American policy in South Vietnam. But that photograph could easily not have been taken. Word had gone out that something exceptional was going to take place in Saigon that day. Yet only one photographer – Malcolm Browne – showed up at the scene. What if he had not? Would Duc have continued his protest? Yes. Of that we can be certain. Would Duc have wanted Browne to stop him? I think not. Duc's intentions were plain and clearly organised. But without Browne present, would Duc's protest have reached the White House? Would President Kennedy have been shocked into making a policy change in South Vietnam? In the case of Degongu, where I was the only outside witness to the attack, the UN camp was in a safe zone twenty kilometres away. If I had put down my camera there, that story would not have been told, at least not in the way that it was told by that picture. And if the story doesn't get told, awareness doesn't get raised; and if you don't have awareness, you're left with ignorance.

PRESENTER: So it's nearly time to hear about your third object, but before we get there, what's next for Tariq Hassan? What are you working on now?

TARIQ: You know, whenever I've held the camera up to my eye, whether that's been in Afghanistan or Libya or Palestine, I've always felt that one eye was focusing on the subject in front of me while the other considers home. So I constantly have this sort of blurring of contexts whereby I imagine superimposing the international context I'm in onto the national context I'm from. I guess that has something to do with audience and my always being aware that my photographs are essentially taken with South Africa in mind. So I imagine, for example, that image of the bullet-ridden theatre in Kabul I described – even though that's not an image I made – but I imagine it being transposed into a South African context and that theatre reappearing somewhere like, I don't know, at the foot of the Union Buildings or at the V&A Waterfront in Cape Town. Or a photograph of a Palestinian refugee camp coming to life in the middle of Sandton. Imagine that. I think that would be my ideal superpower: to transport people into contexts they wouldn't normally be exposed to, to transfer people into the lives and contexts of others. I think we'd have world peace pretty quickly.

I think this constant looking-at-home-from-afar, that distance, has left me with a certain kind of clarity, which is more difficult to get when you're close up. In the case of Kasalia, one of the most striking features of that war for me is the extent of South African involvement in it, especially at the covert level, where the crisis is being fuelled for profit. That is a dimension to the war I'd like to look at more closely because it has everything to do with the insidious relationship between our government and big business, particularly private military and security corporations, which now form such a huge part of our economy.

Presenter: So should we be looking forward to an exposé?

Tariq: Well, we'll have to see. I think one of the things that South Africans have begun to realise is that despite our apparent political transformation to democracy, for most people in this country very little has actually changed. Whatever we say, however the beneficiaries of the current status quo try to rationalise and explain it away, the reality we must accept is that a small elite minority enjoy the post-apartheid dream while the majority continue to languish under the apartheid economic nightmare.

Consider one comparison: The Human Development Index, based on the premise that a country's most valuable resource is its people, is a measure used by the United Nations Development Programme to determine levels of health, education and income in member states. South Africa is ranked at 123 on a list of 187 countries, with life expectancy at birth placed at 52.8 years. Where would you expect to find the Occupied Palestinian Territories – Gaza and the West Bank – on that list, higher or lower than South Africa?

Presenter: Instinctively I'd say lower, but I get the feeling I'd be wrong.

Tariq: You would be. When we begin to see our realities in global terms – the 'big picture', if you like – it really is quite worrying. South Africa is at 123, the OPT is at 114. And with a life expectancy of 72.8 years, Palestinians can expect to live twenty years longer than South Africans.

Now don't get me wrong. I don't deny Palestinians their well-being. That is not the point of my comparison. Rather, what I mean to ask is, why is life expectancy in a free and democratic South Africa twenty years less than in Palestine under the world's longest military occupation?

Presenter: —

Tariq: I'm asking you.

Presenter: I beg your pardon. I thought it was a rhetorical question.

Tariq: On the contrary, it's a very real question and one I want to pose to your listeners too. Why is life expectancy in a free and democratic South Africa twenty years less than in Palestine under the world's longest military occupation? Your fire is hypothetical, but these are real issues and real people are dying. Here's another question. Let's go planetary. Take Johannesburg, the city where we're having this conversation right now. What percentage of all the gold ever mined in the history of this planet came from Johannesburg?

Presenter: I've never taken such a long view of gold mining, so I'm stuck, but let me say that my producer's indicating that the switchboard is lighting up with calls. Unfortunately we don't have time to take calls, but we have an SMS from Ashraf, who says, 'About 40 per cent'.

Tariq: That's right. That's a phenomenal amount of wealth – almost half the world's gold from a single source. And where are those resources going? Who has inherited the earth? We know the answers of the past to questions like these. But what are the answers of the present? I suspect they're the same answers because the economic structures of the past remain the economic structures of the present. Having a black president in South Africa is the same as having a black president in the United States – it's all just surface and veneer, about as genuine as the backdrop of the Paris opera house we spoke about earlier. Remember the old adage 'Don't judge a book by its cover'? That is more pertinent today in South Africa, and for that matter in the United States, than it has ever been. I mean, who continues to control the Johannesburg Stock Exchange, one of the largest in the world and the largest in Africa? These answers we already know. But the rest, the story behind that story, to get to the bottom of that, one first has to get beyond the networks of patronage and the secret cabals and the smoke and mirrors of showpiece legislation that protect the interests of the old guard.

Presenter: Showpiece legislation?

Tariq: Well, I work in conflict zones, so let's take security. It's widely known that South Africa has among the most rigorous laws prohibiting the involvement of its citizens as mercenaries in foreign conflicts, yet despite the blatant involvement of South African citizens in foreign conflicts, there have been no real convictions. Why? Who is benefiting from this flagrant disregard for the law? In South Africa today, just as in Kasalia, you are only guilty until you are proven rich. I'd like to turn my camera to that next.

PRESENTER: You are most famous for your work in conflict zones, though. Would you find it difficult having to adapt to a new paradigm? South Africa isn't a country in conflict.

TARIQ: Isn't it?

PRESENTER: Time to save your final object from the inferno.

TARIQ: Most of my work documents the experiences of people displaced by war and conflict. Of course in this arena one territory looms large – the Occupied Palestinian Territories. Palestinian refugees are the world's largest and oldest refugee population. In 2006, following the election of Hamas, the United States and the European Union imposed sanctions on the Palestinian National Authority. I had been in the Palestinian territories several times before, but circumstances during my stay from 2006 through 2007 were by far the worst and most difficult as sanctions kicked in and the political rivalry between Fatah and Hamas brought Palestinians to the brink of civil war.

Few things demonstrate with greater poignancy how unequal and bizarre and complacent the world can be than a can of sardines I keep on my desk, given to me by a Palestinian refugee during that stay …

From Tariq to Yahya

From: Tariq.Hassan@...
To: Yahya.AlQalaawi@...
Subject: Hi from Tel Aviv
Date: 16 July 2006

Hello my friend. I've arrived in Tel Aviv. I've decided to hire a car here. I'm picking it up in morning, then I'll drive to Ramallah.

I'll call you when I'm through Qalandia checkpoint. Am I coming straight to the office? What's your schedule like for tomorrow?

I'm going to get some sleep.

Tariq

Journal entry

~The West Bank, Saturday 28 October 2006~

In the winter morning kitchen I sift through the sinkful of unwashed dishes for the coffee pot and a glass before huddling sleepily against the old gas stove, numb hands cupped over coffee-brewing flames.

This simple act of making coffee bolsters me. It feels like a conquest. So did lifting a thick head off a soft pillow and then willing a heavy body from a warm bed. I will cajole myself through the morning by ticking off banal achievements as huge triumphs. I tip over a tray, gather the paraphernalia of coffee and smoking, and proceed heavy-limbed to the sun-soaked porch. I pour out a glass, light a cigarette and lean back into thc ample deck sofa. Another victory.

Mornings are the worst, when everything collides like a pile-up on a motorway – the dying flashes of dreams as I wake, the list of tasks for the day, the longing for Leila, the empty water tank, the rumble of gunfire, all travelling at different speeds on different mental frequencies before colliding into the cold light of day. It takes all the will in the world to identify and dislodge oneself from the tangled mess of implication, to free oneself from the wreckage, to scramble to the top of the hill and cry out: 'This is me!'

Eyes mostly closed against the brightness, I commence the cycle of sipping and puffing, sipping and puffing. The stone slabs feel cold under my bare feet, so I swing my legs up onto the sofa and initiate a new cycle of stretching and yawning, stretching and yawning. Sipping and puffing, stretching and yawning – how plentiful are my morning victories.

Not yet thawed, not yet awake, I pour out a second glass of coffee and resume the recline position. Arms stretched out, toes pointed away, back arched to full extent, I let out a loud, growling roar, not quiet birdsong, but nevertheless my own offstage declaration of intent to the world. I have stirred from slumber and am readying once again to play my part this day.

I exhale fully and relax. In the silence following my roar, neighbourly sounds start to filter through fences and over boundary walls: industrious housewives beating rugs, children too young for school plotting their morning games in the sunshine and, from somewhere further away, a radio diffusing the one true virtue of early mornings in Palestine – Fairouz. My ears tune into the abiding melody and filter out the rest, until there is only Fairouz singing only to me. Curling my knees into my chest, I find deep comfort in the familiar refrain, soaking up the promise to shower me with sunlight and clothe me with perfume.

It has been said that a picture is worth a thousand words. But on this trip, I have yet to take that picture. I turn on my computer. My calendar confirms that it is Saturday 28 October. I am a day late with my submission to London. Events have overtaken me. At night I sift through the images I take during the day, but none are even worth keeping, let alone printing. It feels as though circumstances have become too large to be contained in a single frame, too rapid even to be captured at all.

*

Last week Yahya and I were on our way to meet a group of students from Gaza studying at Birzeit University just outside Ramallah. According to Israel, Gazans are now in the West Bank 'illegally'. I was driving, following the road north out of Ramallah, when we hit a flying checkpoint. There was a long queue of cars pulled up on the right, their passengers waiting to have their papers inspected by the soldiers up ahead. I slowed down to join the queue.

'Carry on driving,' Yahya instructed.

'Are you crazy?'

'Do as I say. Stay in the left lane and carry on slowly. Trust me.'

It was the most counter-intuitive thing I've ever done, driving past a row of parked cars on the right and up towards a heavily armed checkpoint. As we approached the soldiers, I was convinced that they would open fire.

'Slow down,' Yahya said, 'and flash the headlights once.'

I noticed the Palestinians who had been made to stand by the side of the road. But I did as Yahya had instructed, slowed down and flashed the headlights.

Two soldiers turned towards our car.

'Keep coasting,' Yahya said.

I don't think I was breathing, but I kept coasting.

The soldiers were now right in front of the car. If I kept coasting, I would run into them.

'Now wave at them,' Yahya said. 'Like this.'

I raised my hand and waved just as he had done. The soldiers nodded, stepped aside and waved us through.

*

Yahya does not say anything. He just sits there staring ahead. I'm expecting an explanation, but he does not offer one. This annoys me.

'What the fuck, Yahya? So you're just going to sit there now.'

He gave me a clouded look, as though I'd woken him from a deep sleep. 'What do you want me to say?' he asked.

'What just happened back there?'

Yahya gestured to the front of the car. 'Israeli plates' was all he said.

'Israeli plates? That's your explanation? You are Palestinian. I am South African. But you made us drive past a queue of Palestinians waiting at a checkpoint because we have Israeli plates? Fuck, Yahya. There were women and children back there!'

Yahya said nothing. He reached for his cellphone. 'You're going to turn left up ahead. The house is just along there. I'll let them know we're here.'

I stopped the car.

'What are you doing?' Yahya asked. 'That's the house over there.'

'Yahya, I'm so fucking angry with you right now, just ...' I banged my palms against the steering wheel and got out of the car.

Inside the car, Yahya was on the phone speaking to the Gazans. I heard him explain that we were in the white car with the Israeli plates pulled up by the side of the road. I heard him qualify that it was a hire car I had picked up in Tel Aviv. I heard him explain that I was not feeling well, which was why I was pacing around trying to get some fresh air. This made me even more annoyed. He said that we'd be up at the house in a few minutes. Then he got out of the car, lit a cigarette and leaned against the bonnet.

'So, what? You would have felt nobler for waiting in that queue? Or what, you feel like a collaborator for driving through, for taking abusive privileges?'

I looked at Yahya, but I could not speak.

'Go on. Tell me. Do you think I've robbed you of a "real" Palestinian checkpoint experience? And you're upset, because why? Because you can't send an email to Johannesburg tonight about how difficult the situation is and how you had to stand in a queue at a checkpoint for one, two, three, four, five, six hours or however long those people are going to be kept there? Fuck that! What difference would you have made to those people standing there?'

'Those people! Those people? What about solidarity, Yahya? What about togetherness and joining in the reality?'

He swung around and pointed into the distance. 'You see way over there. That's Tel Aviv.'

Then he swung round again. 'And over there, that's Jerusalem.'

Then he walked up to me. 'I can't go to either. But you have been to both. You want the real Palestinian experience? You want to demonstrate solidarity? Deny yourself those privileges, then come stand here and look at the forbidden horizon. And the young men waiting to meet you in that house? Some of them have not seen their families in Gaza for nearly ten years. They're bright young men, but they live low-key lives here, hiding from Israeli soldiers who'll send them back to Gaza, steering clear of Palestinian officials in the West Bank who think they're Hamas scum. You want a real Palestinian experience? Surrender your travel documents and go and live with them. Don't fucking preach to me about solidarity. I don't have time for this shit. They're waiting. Let's go.'

I photographed the Gazan students. I photographed the house they shared. When we left, I photographed Tel Aviv on the 'forbidden horizon', as Yahya had called it. I even photographed the hire car with its Israeli plates, but none of those photographs conveyed the story of that day. My camera can't capture what I see or what I'm told, and the pictures I take during the day only end up in my recycle bin at night.

'A toast to our host,' Yahya declared last night, clinking his glass against the bottle and encouraging us into Statue of Liberty poses, with glasses raised to the night. 'To Tariq, may he drink more and photograph better.'

Yahya proceeded to proffer variations of the toast to suit the pursuits of all those present in clockwise order of their seating around the porch.

'Marwan, may he drink more, teach better ...

Farid, may he drink more, drive better ... Said, may he drink more, nurse better ... Nadir, may he drink more, design better ... Mazin, may he drink more, be unemployed better ... Me, Yahya, may I drink more, coordinate better ... and finally, our brother Zachariah here next to me, may he especially drink more, play better and make us all forget totally how fucking ghastly life can be', which prompted Zach to conjure an old favourite by plucking the strings of his *oud* and everybody else to join in the song.

It was nearly dawn when Zach put down his *oud* and our night together was over. An uneasy silence descended on our party. Furtive glances flitted around the porch as each tried to avoid eyes they had known for decades. Some leaned forward, resting elbows awkwardly on knees; some leaned back to search the ceiling for whatever might be concealed up there; some remained immobile, staring vacantly at anything that would not stare back.

His absence had struck me again when Yahya was making his round of toasts. He wasn't running late. He hadn't forgotten. As Yahya was making his bespoke clockwise toasts, I wondered one thing: which of Fadi's pursuits would Yahya have toasted – and immediately realised another: that Fadi would never again be amongst us, not since we laid him to rest earlier that day in a hastily dug grave.

When the mourners started to disperse, we lingered, seeking out one another, until it was just us gathered in a stunned and silent circle around the grave. The silence followed us from Fadi's grave to the big tree at the bottom of my garden. There we took up our usual places in a circle of stones as we had done so many times before. Someone set the fire and, during our silent contemplation of the flames, people disappeared in turns to reappear a short while later with offerings for the night: Mazin with bread and meat for the fire, Nadir with beer and arak. But it wasn't until Zach returned with his life-asserting *oud* that proceedings started to assume the reassuring shape of the many happier gatherings we'd shared underneath this old tree – Farid's discharge from hospital, Said's marriage, Mazin's release from prison.

Hours later, when there was no more wood for the fire, we brewed coffee in the embers and moved to the porch. Here Zach strummed gentler tunes until Yahya initiated his round of improvised toasts, which for a while pulled us back from sorrow, but when it was complete, returned us all to silence.

I looked at the circle of faces around the porch, friends who had known one another all their lives. Sometimes the circle contracted, like when Nadir gave in to wanderlust and travelled the world. Sometimes the circle was buckled, like when Mazin was sent to an Israeli prison and Farid into a coma when his taxi sped into a head-on collision with a truck. Sometimes it became distorted, like when Marwan disappeared into despair after the father he had never met died in exile, or when Said was plummeted into the overwhelming role of young widower and single parent after his wife was shot dead when she ran out of the house during a curfew to fetch their toddler who had wandered into the street. Whatever the catastrophe, they have always shape-shifted their way through tragedy, always returning to reconstitute the circle. But now, as we sat silently in a circle of sorrow, the truth we were conceding was that tonight, with Fadi's death, one amongst us had left, never to return.

I compose a cover email to London. 'I'm sorry for the delay ... Unexpected circumstances ... I am pleased to attach ...'

I attach my piece. I decided to call it '... And 1 Can of Sardines' because, really, what a fucking joke.

I also attach a selection of images – the road to Atouf, mobile phones on the dark streets of Zbouba, and the can of sardines.

I sign off:

Sincerely,

Tariq Hassan

Relay: Kas/Cairo

A hideously rutted road, a constant thoroughfare for Israeli tanks and military vehicles, runs for twelve kilometres northwest of Jenin to the village of Zbouba. Since the Wall, Zbouba has become the northernmost village in what remains of the West Bank. With the area having lost most of its land and wells, the local economy lies in tatters. The village has no functioning electricity supply and its alternative source of water in the Al-Gard Valley has been polluted by overflowing effluent from a nearby Israeli military camp. Some homes have generators, but as sanctions claw deeper into empty pockets, most households can no longer afford to run them. Multiple adaptors wait in wall sockets so that cellphones can be charged in the event of sporadic supply. At night their illuminated screens cast a blue hue on faces in the otherwise dark streets …

This is ANA in Harare, Khartoum, Abuja, Kinshasa and across Africa on TV, on radio and online.

The recent convictions of Thomas Lubanga Dyilo and Charles Taylor for war crimes by the International Criminal Court in The Hague have finally secured justice for their victims in the Democratic Republic of Congo and Liberia. They have also brought to two the total number of ICC convictions to date. A further twenty-four people continue to face charges for crimes against humanity by the Court. All, like Dyilo and Taylor, are African. While the ICC deserves praise for the convictions of Dyilo and Taylor, in a new series of programmes presented by Tanya Wood, ANA investigates the partial nature of international justice. With only one Arab state – Jordan – having ratified the treaty, we ask: How international is international justice when Indonesia, Turkey, Egypt, Iran, Israel, India, Pakistan, Russia, China and, perhaps most notably, the US have yet to ratify the treaty? What, if anything, can be done to secure their participation? And with Britain having ratified the treaty, can we expect to see Tony Blair in The Hague too? That's Uneven Justice *with Tanya Wood every Monday morning at nine and Wednesday evenings at seven.*

But first here on Radio ANA, South Africa's Anti-Mercenary Act of 2006 and Foreign Military Assistance Act of 1998 are widely hailed as the most rigorous legislation of their kind anywhere in the world. Still, South African citizens remain actively involved in military and security roles in almost all the world's major combat zones, including Libya, Afghanistan and Iraq. But there are very few prosecutions and even fewer convictions. Coming up next on ANA, Gabriel Audigier presents The Short Arm of the Law …

'My old boat and my old river'

'Are you hungry?' Yahya asked when we had finished our drinks.

I nodded.

'Good. I have an idea.'

We took the elevator down to the lobby. I followed Yahya to the hotel deli, where he made a careful selection of cheese and fruit and bread before leading me to the door.

'Let's go,' he said.

Out on the street, he guided me deftly through the traffic, clutching me with one hand and our picnic with the other. 'Crossing skills,' he called it. 'Essential in Cairo.'

When we arrived at an embankment overhung by trees, he paused, as if to acknowledge our sudden seclusion and elicit my consent to proceed. I reached down to adjust my ankle strap and make a quick assessment.

It seemed very dark down there, yet Tariq trusted Yahya so I felt I had to do the same. I straightened myself, pushed back my hair and let Yahya lead me down the narrow flight of cobbled stairs that lead to the river. When we stepped onto the embankment, I smiled. We had come to a little harbour where feluccas bobbed up and down in the water that lapped the riverbank. No sooner had we arrived than we were surrounded by boisterous boatmen competing for our custom. Yahya made a quick transaction and soon we were out in the middle of the river floating under a large white sail that flapped gently in the breeze.

It struck me then that I had never been on a boat, that this was my first time out on the water. In distance we had not come far, but it felt as though Yahya had transported me to a different world where the lights of the city sparkled on the surface of a liquid screen. I watched him banter with the helmsman, the two of them slapping hands in animated appreciation of a joke. Out on the river, the anxiety I'd felt since Tariq's departure for the Libyan border started to ebb away. I reached out to touch the surface of the water. If I continued to fret, I would be undermining the faith and trust that Tariq, Yahya and their associates place in one another. We had only been married a year, but it was now clear to me that I was going to have to abandon the role of paranoid wife if I was going to be any good at this.

When we had eaten, the helmsman handed me the rudder; then he and Yahya reclined to smoke.

'Where shall I go?' I asked.

Yahya translated.

'I'm a poor man,' the helmsman replied. 'All my father left me is this old boat and this even older river. You have crossed a great distance to be a guest under my sail tonight. Now you have to set your own course. My old boat and my old river, these are my gifts to you for the night. Take them and go wherever you like.'

I took hold of the rudder, sensing the force of the river running up my arm. I strengthened my grip and started setting course through a very ancient current.

*

On the walk back to my hotel, we stopped to buy tea from a street vendor who had set his cart halfway across one of the bridges that spanned the Nile. The wind was blowing from the north, following the course of the river.

Yahya suggested that we sit facing south. 'It's good to have the wind at your back.'

During our looping conversations through the course of the evening, it had become clear to me that while I knew little of Yahya's world, he was very well informed about mine.

'Libya's behind us now.' He smiled reassuringly. 'Just in case you're still wondering ... And South Africa is ahead, that way. A very long way ahead.'

I sipped my tea. It was very sweet.

'In all ways a very long way ahead,' Yahya continued, as though speaking to himself. And then he turned to face me.

'Do you know that, if I'm honest, I expected Palestine would be free before South Africa?' he said.

It was clearly a legitimate parallel to Yahya, though I couldn't see the connection. I did not know what it had been prefixed upon.

'Why is that?' I asked.

He shrugged his shoulders. 'Because the PLO is so much richer than the ANC? Because the PLO funded the ANC? I suppose with that came the assumption ...'

Yahya trailed off but brought himself back quickly,

as though he had neglected his role as host.

'We admire your achievements,' he said. 'And perhaps, if we're honest, envy them a little too.'

I did not know what to make of Yahya's comments, or of Yahya. I work with patients and syringes. I fight illness and try to cure diseases. Those are my day-to-day concerns. I realised that I had come to resent the world beyond my own, because that world drew Tariq away from me. Sipping sweet tea over the Nile, I had to confront the people beyond my horizon, people like Yahya, who knew so much more about my world than I had ever bothered to learn about theirs. What would I do next? Continue to shut them out? Continue to resent the world I did not know? Would I continue to shut Yahya out and resent him too?

*

Back at my hotel, the receptionist waved a note in the air.

'Madam, you had a telephone call.'

It was a message from Tariq. He'd arrived safely at the Libyan border.

Yahya smiled. 'Now you can sleep easy. Good night, Leila. You have my number. Call me if you need anything.'

I nodded and turned towards the lift. I pressed the button and waited for it to descend.

'Leila.' He had spoken my name hesitantly, just above a whisper.

I turned around. There was Yahya, looking uncertain.

'Would you like to have dinner with me tomorrow night?'

The lift arrived. I stepped inside and pressed the button.

'That would be lovely, thank you.'

Somewhere

I fell asleep feeling hungry. I woke feeling hungrier still. When did I last eat? Was it morning, afternoon or night? Should I be feeling hungry? Or is this being greedy? My waking thoughts were to go to the fridge and rummage for leftovers. I stumbled to the kitchen, my eyes still full of sleep. I bumped into the fridge, the thud resounding strangely, less like metal, more like brick. It roused me from sleep. I opened my eyes to find myself staring at the white surface of the fridge, but standing too close to open the door without also knocking myself to the ground. I stepped back to reach for the handle. I found myself standing here, staring at this blank white wall.

I must try to remember what I remember because remembering is all I have. I must rehearse and catalogue my stories in my head because my head is all I have.

I remember Leila offering to print the final version of my speech while I took a shower. I remember the water bursting onto my face. I remember thinking that that was a good thing because it would help clear my eyes and wake me up. It had been a late night. I had given an interview in the afternoon before moving on to dinner in the evening, where I had had a lot to drink. I remember ordering crème brûlée for dessert because I wanted something sweet to freshen my mouth. I don't remember eating it, though. What I would give to have that crème brûlée now.

I remember the waiter coming to say that our cars were ready. I remember our party rising from the long table. Without us seated there, the restaurant seemed suddenly empty. I remember leaving the restaurant surrounded by people, but with Leila by my side. I remember the two of us giggling in the back seat during the drive through the city and back to our hotel. I remember us kissing in the lift, then me walking funny down the corridor. I remember our bursting into laughter the moment we entered our room. I remember us falling onto the bed. I remember us making urgent, fully clothed love.

I remember waking with the curtains open and the room already bright. Leila was in the shower. I reached to check the time, then stumbled out of bed to fumble at my computer, a headache surfacing right between my eyes. I ordered coffee, then started to edit my speech, inputting the revisions I'd jotted down in my pocketbook during the rush from this engagement to that:

- South Africa's widely hailed Anti-Mercenary Act drawn up in 2006 remains to be written into law.
- Executive procrastination is the reason for the delay.
- In the case of Equatorial Guinea, it is now known that the South African government knew about the planned coup at least six

months beforehand but did nothing to stop it.
- President Jacob Zuma's stance can be judged from his comment that the perpetrators of the coup in Equatorial Guinea have been released because President Nguema had learnt from President Mandela how to forgive.

I remember Leila emerging in clouds from the steaming bathroom, looking like a newly dispatched angel, all tucked up in white. I remember her jumping when there was a knock on the door behind her.

'Coffee,' I explained.

I rose to get the door while she slipped back into the bathroom.

When I'd signed for the coffee, I joined her in the bathroom and tried to seduce her while she was drying her hair.

'You have work to do,' she said, feigning a schoolmarm accent, which caused me to snort a laugh.

'I've done it, miss,' I lied.

'But I've just had a shower,' she protested. 'And we'll be late for lunch.'

'Have another. You've missed a spot,' I teased, touching her nipples and pulling her into the shower with me. 'Lunch won't start without us.'

I remember our siesta after lunch. How perfect it was, how tired we both were, how deliciously we flopped onto the bed, thankful to be alone once again, asleep before our heads even hit our pillows. I remember waking when the coffee I had asked to be brought up at five was delivered. If I had known that was to be the last time I would wake with Leila lying in my arms, I would have set the coffee aside and gone back to sleep. I poured us each a cup. While we leaned against the headboard sipping, Leila ran her hand down my thigh and patted my knee.

'Ready for tonight?'

Ready for tonight? I wonder if that question hounds Leila like it hounds me.

I nodded and kissed her on the forehead. 'Thank you for coming.'

'You're welcome,' she said. 'It might surprise you, but I've had a lovely time.'

'Have you really?' I asked, slipping my hand under the sheet and cupping her breast. 'Even out of bed?'

She laughed a throaty laugh. 'Later,' she promised, brushing my hand aside.

'When?'

'After your speech.'

'Immediately after,' I suggested. 'Before the goddamn dinner. Please. I think I know the perfect backstage spot.'

'You demon.'

'But we'll have to do it standing up.'

'You obsessed beggar,' she laughed.

'Go on,' I winked. 'Spare a dime.'

'Okay, enough of this,' Leila declared, setting down her cup. 'You'd better jump into the shower. I'll print out your stuff.'

If I'd known that would be the last time my hand would cup her breasts, I would have flung my computer through the window, cancelled the evening's event and taken her back to bed.

RELAY: CAIRO/ADDIS ABABA

Zbouba's proximity to Israel exposes two contrasting worlds. I visited at the height of summer when fridges stood open and fans stood still. The coldest thing in the village was resentment. From his rooftop, my host pointed through the twilight at a distant hill on the other side of the Wall.

'All the land from here to that hill is ours. But this wall has taken it. I can't go there any more. And look,' he said, pointing at Israel. 'Their lights are coming on but here we are in darkness. Our roads are broken from their tanks, but see how their cars fly by on their motorways. How many international laws has Israel broken? Here, right in front of us, right next to my house, is one,' he said, indicating the Wall. 'And this war in Lebanon now, how many people is Israel killing? Israel makes war – Bush and Blair say nothing. We vote – we get sanctions.'

I remember Leila fixing my black tie. I remember me looping her pendant around her neck and struggling with the clasp. I remember thinking: 'How grown-up we've become.' I remember the knock at the door, my guide, or chaperone, or escort – I never really know what to call the posse of people who come to fuss around me at such events. I remember us walking in a triangle down the carpeted corridor, my escort in front, Leila and I following behind. We stepped into the lift. How silent the world became once the doors had sealed shut.

Lift descending.

My stomach turned. I inhaled deeply, trying to make it settle. I remember Leila taking my hand and squeezing it tight.

'You'll be fine,' she whispered.

I looked up at the numbers that seemed to me like a countdown looming above our heads: 5, 4, 3, 2, 1.

You'll be fine. I wonder if those words haunt Leila as much as they haunt me. How oblivious, how unsuspecting we were in that plush hushed lift descending us straight to hell.

RELAY: ADDIS ABABA/ISTANBUL

Seventeen kilometres northeast of Nablus lies one of Palestine's oldest traumas, Al Fara'a Refugee Camp, one of nineteen officially recognised camps in the West Bank and fifty-nine in haemorrhaging Gaza and the Middle East. All were set up after the Arab–Israeli War of 1948, when 750 000 Palestinians were expelled from their cities, towns and villages following the creation of the state of Israel. Palestinian refugees now constitute the largest and oldest single refugee community in the world.

While most camps are situated in or near towns and cities, Al Fara'a is a rural camp. This has implications for access to work, secondary and higher education, water and health. In June 2002, eleven-year-old Mohammad Eshtewi was struck by a tear-gas canister fired from an Israeli tank. He required oxygen, but the camp clinic was closed. With road closures and checkpoints, it takes one and a half hours to travel seventeen kilometres to Nablus. By the time an ambulance arrived, Mohammad was dead ...

I remember the doors sliding open. I remember a

crowded lobby. I remember Edith Piaf's voice singing, as I had requested, a little something for Leila. The Little Sparrow was her favourite singer. I could be cheesy like that.

They came in hand in hand
Why can't I forget?
For they'd seen the sign
That said: Room to let
The sunshine of love
Was deep in their eyes
So young, oh so young
Too young to be wise

When Leila registered the tune, she flashed me a smile. If I'd known that would be the last time I'd see her smile, I would have held her face in my hands and never let go. I remember my chaperone holding the button to keep the doors from closing. I gestured to Leila to step out first. She did, like a diamond into the light. I saw our host for the evening approaching.

'Dr Mashal, you look perfectly radiant tonight.'

I remember him handing Leila over to the bevy of waiting wives. I remember thinking: 'She's going to hate that.' I remember him turning his attention back to me. I was surprised by the sudden look of horror on his face. Was I still looking dreadfully hungover and not as radiant as my wife? And then it felt as though the world had clicked into slow motion … I felt a thing against my head. I felt a thing over my mouth. I became completely surrounded. I could not see my host. I could no longer see my wife.

'Leila! Leila!' was what I was shouting through the thing covering my mouth.

My feet were scrambling desperately towards her, but my heels were only dragging uselessly on the ground.

'Leila! Leila!' I shouted, but all I could hear was the sound of my screams resounding muffled in my ears and sounding more like 'Heyher! Heyher!'

I now know that the thing at my head was a gun and the thing over my mouth was a leather-gloved hand. They were the last things I caught sight of as I was thrown into the back seat of a car, a hood pulled over my head before the door had even been slammed shut.

Relay: Istanbul/Karakas

In 1949 the United Nations established the United Nations Relief and Works Agency (UNRWA) to deal specifically with the Palestinian refugees. Since then the agency has become synonymous with providing services for them. However lamentable their political plight, governments and popular opinion remain reassured that, on humanitarian grounds, the Palestinian refugees are cared for by the United Nations.

But nearly six decades later, unemployment in the camps remains high and the majority of the refugee population are unable to live independently of relief aid. Graduates queue for menial work in the agency's emergency work programme, which pays two dollars a day and provides work for only six months. Schools are overcrowded and services for women – the backbone of refugee society – children, the disabled, the youth and the elderly are rudimentary. As the agency's funding crisis deepens, camp residents are forced into greater hardship, their only safety net being the concern and generosity of their neighbours ...

EDITH'S SMASHING GLASS

'The severity of the moment.' That was how one witness had put it.

One never imagines that such a thing could happen, something that pulls the plug out of your world, sucking you out of yourself like water down the drain, pulling you away from everything happening around you. And when it does, what could be worse than it happening when you are entirely surrounded by a bunch of scrutinising self-important bigots? How can you shout and scream, how can you dig at your eyes and pull in desperation at your hair when you are far away from friends and governed completely by an instinct that advises composure and poise at all times, no matter what?

I suppose it was inevitable. In my own life I was Leila Mashal. I knew what that meant and so did Tariq. He had no need for a Leila Hassan fussing around him just as I had no wish for a Tariq Mashal sitting on my head. But here, in the midst of this grand gathering, surrounded by these eminent people, however much they said to me Dr Mashal this and Dr Mashal that, I sensed immediately that I had stirred resentment just by walking into the room. Perhaps if I'd been dowdy, perhaps then they might have felt at liberty to indulge what I suspect must be their constant supposition – that nobody can know the man of the moment better, nobody can be more appealing to him than they, least of all the frump he was with. But as things were, I had unsettled their assumptions and I could not believe how quickly, how blatantly they made it clear that my punishment was now being meted out. An awful calamity had just befallen them – the star of their show snatched right from their very midst, before most of them had even had a glimpse. I was the one now stranded in their pond, but as I was not dowdy Mrs Hassan, they could withhold their lifeline while they pressed keypads to broadcast their catastrophe, some even glancing at me as they lifted their phones to their ears, because they were dealing with their emergency, and in the meanwhile, Leila Mashal, well, it seemed as though she was going to have to wait.

To be honest, I wasn't taking in a word any of them were saying. I had expected Tariq to be separated from me at some point during the reception, but I imagined that this would arise naturally out the dynamics of the event, once we had been offered something to drink, once we had eased into the atmosphere of the room a little bit. I was not prepared for Tariq to be whisked immediately from me the moment we stepped into the lobby. I had to make a quick revision as clearly no concessions would be made for the 'us' that binds Tariq and me. I realised that this was not going to be one of those joyful convivial events, which in the end escalates into a delightfully egalitarian free-for-all, but rather a terribly old-fashioned convocation of the pompous, in which a strict hierarchy applied, devoid of all the nuances, animations and pleasures of life. I began to realise that Tariq and I had stepped into a reception at which our hosts would only be pretending to sip at champagne cocktails, after which we would be ushered into the auditorium where he would deliver his televised address that a whole country waited to hear, after which there would still be the gala dinner to get through. It began to become apparent that, during all of this, Tariq and I would be kept strictly separated from each other, with him firmly in the clutches of the expert men who read him while I was to be held on a tight leash by their boring prudish wives. Any inkling that I was with Tariq, any suggestion that he might have a life outside the parameters in which they knew him, was strictly to be underplayed, overlooked and suppressed. It was then that I remembered two things: one, the backstage spot that Tariq had mentioned, and I decided that when I was next beside him, I would ask him to point it out so that I could go and wait there for him; and two, I had completely forgotten to collect his address from the printer before we left our room.

I felt myself being passed into a circle of stern-eyed women whose leader embarked on the only conversation she ever made, introducing her companions one by one. I did not register any of their names because my mind was still with Tariq and my ears still tuned to the Little Sparrow singing sweetly into them.

They wanted a place
A small hideaway
A place of their own
If just for one day

'How grown-up this is,' Tariq had said while I fixed his tie, reaching from behind around his broad shoulders while he stood facing the mirror. I stood on tiptoes to rest my chin on his shoulder. When our eyes met in the mirror he winked at me.

'Thank you,' he said.

'You're welcome,' I replied, feeling his strong chest expand beneath his starched shirt as I stroked his tie into place.

'Not for the tie,' he said.

'You have more than that to thank me for?'

'Well, for the tie too, but also for everything else.'

'Oh, Tariq,' I smiled.

'No, I mean it, Leila. Thank you for everything, for keeping me going, for keeping us going, for enduring the poverty. And the pain.'

The walls were so bare
The carpets so thin
But they took that room
And heaven walked in

'And, you might add, for proofing your speech one last time and picking out loads more mistakes while you were in the shower!'

'Really,' he exclaimed as I swung him around.

'Yes, really. Now here, show you're truly thankful and do my pendant.'

He took the pendant from my hand as I stood facing the desk, reminding myself to collect the printed lecture from the tray to hand to his escort when she arrived. But then Tariq said something that unsettled me a little because it was not like him to say such things.

'I couldn't bear to be separated from you, not even

for a day. I think I would lose my mind.'

So I turned around to face him.

'Wait a minute,' he exclaimed. 'I'm struggling with the clasp … Okay, done.'

I looked up at him. 'Whatever makes you say such a thing? Nothing's going to separate us, except perhaps your adoring "public" waiting anxiously downstairs.'

*

Once all the women had been introduced, a waiter offered a silver tray into the centre of our circle. We each took a glass but, before he left, I beckoned him closer and whispered that he please inform Tariq's escort to collect his speech from the printer in our room. I slipped him the key.

'Certainly, madam,' he obliged as I returned my attention to the group.

'So, you do the running around for him, do you?' one of the wives remarked. Perhaps she was trying to be friendly, but I thought it an inquisitive comment after I had so clearly tried to be discreet.

'Not at all,' I countered. 'I only helped out with the printing because Tariq's no good with technology.'

She raised her chin at me while sliding her eyes down my dress. And then I panicked for a moment, imagining the headlines in the morning papers: 'Tariq Hassan No Good With Technology'. I drank from my glass, then ran the tip of my forefinger around the rim.

Shine another glass
Make the hours pass

'He is certainly proving to be rather popular,' another

of the women observed.

By 'he' I assumed she meant Tariq, and in 'rather' I detected a hint of disapproval and a tinge of surprise. She tilted her head around me to get a better view, which left me feeling as though I were a little in the way.

'Good heavens. He's being completely swamped.'

Not wanting to seem keen, I determined not to turn around and play the admiring wife, but snatched the opportunity of another swig while all their heads were turned to face the door.

'Gosh, there really is a pile-up to get at him. Is it like this everywhere he goes?'

The question caught me in the midst of another gulp, the bubbly contents splashing in the glass as I moved it quickly away from my mouth, a drop flying up to catch me on the nose.

'Oops! Bubbles,' I exclaimed, then quickly brushed away the drop. But I knew I'd been caught at it and watched as disapproving eyes darted quickly around the circle. The women, following their leader's lead, lifted their still full glasses simultaneously to their lips, but hardly took a sip. It was becoming clear to me that no conversation was going to erupt here without my having to initiate it. I was hurriedly trying to formulate a question – 'What do you do?' – before deciding better of it, when one of them made to speak. Relieved, I anticipated her contribution.

'What a peculiar choice of music, don't you think?'

It was clear that the question had not been posed to me, because she did not meet my eyes when she looked around for a response. I looked down at the bubbles breaking on the surface of what remained of my champagne, pondering whether to take another sip or just to swig the whole damn lot, and that is what I was doing, staring into the remnants of my glass, when somebody tapped me on the shoulder.

'Dr Mashal,' I heard the voice say. 'Professor Hassan has just been kidnapped.'

We found them next day
The way they had planned
So white, so cold
But still hand in hand
The sunshine of love
Was all they possessed
And so in the sunshine
We laid them to rest.

Unless we work with them, it is difficult to visualise our spouses in their professional capacity. 'Professor Hassan.' I was not used to hearing the man I called Tariq being referred to as that. The title was new. And the word 'kidnap', an act so alien, so seemingly irrelevant to my life, added yet further to the absurdity of the announcement such that at first I wondered why this man thought the information pertinent to me. Then I felt my mind split in two, one half repeating what had just been reported – Professor Hassan has been kidnapped – the other processing, interpreting and translating the news for me – Professor Hassan, the man you call Tariq, the man who is your husband, has been kidnapped. I looked up at the messenger, not registering a face. But that's impossible, I thought. He made love to me in the shower this morning. I can still feel him inside me now. We have a clandestine rendezvous at a secret backstage spot.

They sleep side by side
Two children alone
And I'm sure they've found
A place of their own
So why must I see
The ribbon she wore
The glow on his face
When I closed the door?

Relay: Karakas/Rome

Since 1949, and in the absence of an imminent solution, the UNRWA mandate has been repeatedly renewed. But with each passing year, the situation compounds. Camps like Al Fara'a stand on land leased from private landowners for ninety nine years. This land area is finite and boundaries are strictly defined. While Israeli settlements continue to mushroom and swell illegally across the West Bank, refugee camps, whatever their population increase, are not allowed to expand outwards. The populations of the camps now exceed capacity. While children in settlements play in swimming pools and gardens, children in camps play in the confines of their overcrowded homes or in the narrow streets of the camp. In Al Fara'a, where half the population is under eighteen, the nursery school is in the sunless basement of the mosque. Domestic space is at a premium. With around seven occupants per floor, a single three-storey building accommodates about twenty-five people. Throughout the Middle East, Palestinian refugees live in concrete labyrinths three storeys high, one for each generation born in exile, causing camps to take on the semblance of lopsided cities and the supposedly temporary to manifest increasingly as the potentially permanent.

While families have paid personally to extend their homes, they do not own the land on which the houses stand. This leaves them without the privileges and options that usually benefit homeowners. They cannot sell their houses, and if for any reason homes stand empty for more than six months, they are liable to be confiscated. While Israel encourages settlers from India into subsidised settlements, Palestinian refugees remain captive, tied to their camps. A fourth generation is being born, but buildings are too weak to accommodate a fourth floor. Where will the next generation of Palestinian refugees go? The lease on camp land expires in 2047.

*

'What!'

The shrill exclamation from the leader of the women startled me. My eyes moved in their sockets, but my body stood rooted to the spot. I watched the circle of women into whose midst I had been deposited disintegrate as they all struggled to get around me and ahead of each other to join the commotion at the front door, leaving me completely alone with only Edith to comfort me, just as Tariq had intended.

Be still children still
Your shadows may start
The tears in my eyes
And tears in my heart

I watched a waiter return a tray of empty glasses through a service entrance now visible at the back of that now vacated corner of the room. The door remained open behind him for a moment and I was able to see the industry in the kitchen before the door swung shut.

Shine another glass
Let the hours pass
Working every day
In a cheap café
Everything is fine
Till I see that sign
How can I forget?
It says: Room to let.

RELAY: ROME/MADRID

Part of Al Fara'a's southern boundary is formed by its graveyard. During the worst of times, this seems an apt place to conclude. On Friday 27 October 2006, Fadi Soboh was shot in the heart by Israeli soldiers during a raid on the camp. He was unarmed. He was twenty-five. He was a son. He was a grandson. He was a brother. He was a nephew. He was a cousin. And he was my friend. But to that soldier who shot to kill, he was only another Palestinian target. Fadi died as he was born, a refugee in his own land. He was buried in Al Fara'a's southern graveyard, another Palestinian setting burdened with wincing symbolism. By 1996, it had become full, forcing the refugees of Al Fara'a to add a layer of topsoil over existing graves. The day after he was killed, Fadi was laid to rest here, buried in death as he had lived in life, in an overcrowded graveyard, which, like his family home, is extending upward, eternally, on borrowed land and shaky foundations, until one day, one possible outcome is achieved ... It all falls down.

As the tune wound down into distorted chords, twisted

rhythms and the sound of smashing glass, I started to feel Tariq slip away from me like a receding ocean. I was standing alone in the middle of the room, but I couldn't think of what to do about it. So I continued to stand, holding my empty glass. I would have rested it on a table, but they all seemed so far away and walking was not yet something I felt I could do. I saw a waiter approach. I recognised his face, but I could not place him exactly.

'I hope madam does not mind,' he started hesitantly. 'The professor's escort said she was busy and told me to fetch the professor's lecture from the room.'

I nodded.

'But the problem is, madam …' He hesitated before proceeding. 'The problem is that when I got there the room had been ransacked and there was no paper in the printer. I have told the professor's escort and also the manager of the hotel. He has taken the madam's key. I'm sorry, madam. Can I take the madam's glass?'

'Thank you' was all I could think of to say as I passed the glass into his white-gloved hand. I watched him walk away. When he had disappeared through the service door, I turned to face the commotion at the entrance. I remembered the first words that had been said to me when I entered the lobby: 'Dr Mashal, you look perfectly radiant tonight.' I glanced at my wristwatch. It couldn't have been more than ten minutes since those words were spoken, but standing there alone, watching Tariq's public fall into panic and dismay, those minutes already seemed to stretch like years behind me and I wondered whether I was still bearing up. I started to finger the diamond that dangled from the chain around my neck, the diamond which Tariq had hung there, but which he was no longer in the room to see sparkle. While my fingers fiddled with the diamond, my ears started to resound with the echo of distorted chords as Edith's song wound down into twisted rhythms and ended with the sound of smashing glass.

Relay: Rome/New Delhi

Until that day, why concern ourselves too excessively with the plight of Palestinian refugees living in camps like Al Fara'a? With the refugees having no right to return to their ancestral lands in Israel and having in the intervening sixty years grown into the world's oldest and largest refugee population, we can take comfort that the occupants of camps like Al Fara'a will be cared for by UNRWA. Consider current UNRWA food relief rations for three people every four months:

- 30 kg flour
- 2 kg lentils
- 2 kg sugar
- 2 kg rice
- 1 kg powdered milk
- and 1 can of sardines

Tariq Hassan
The West Bank
October 2006

From Leila to Yahya

From: Leila.Mashal@...
To: Yahya.AlQalaawi@...
Subject: Statement
Date: 14 August 20—

Dear Yahya,
It appears I won't be able to make the statement you requested. The authorities here have advised me against commenting publicly for the time being as this might jeopardise their investigations and compromise Tariq's safety.

Do you remember that night in Cairo all those years ago? I asked you a question: 'Where is Libya?', which you answered with a question: 'Missing him already?'

We have local elections in South Africa next year. I'm thinking of standing. I don't expect to win, but it would be one way of injecting the issues raised by Tariq's abduction into the political agenda. I don't know. What do you think?
Leila

PART II

Omens are wont to reside in beginnings.

– Janus, Roman god of beginnings

Somewhere

I'm thinking again about beginnings, about the beginning. Why does it haunt me so? I don't know, but this is what I'm thinking: If the beginning was the word, then tell, from whose non-existent mouth did it proceed? For do words not have prerequisites; do they not rely on systems? Are words not preceded by thoughts? And thoughts, do they not depend on something with which to think them? To be articulated – the metamorphosis of thought into word – if to be recorded for posterity, will there not have been pre-assembled mechanisms of sound, symbols for representation? All this invisible scaffolding propping up beginnings – apparent beginnings – the fundamental rules of obviousness obscured by the concealing proclamations of holy writ. I ask about these now, while my mind is nimble and I can still feel it pulsing in my head ... Unless, of course, the asking is already a sign, not of mental agility, but of psychological decay. How would I know? The untethered mind can lose its civilisation. It can become self-absorbed and incorrect.

What I do know is this: I've lost faith in glossy beginnings. Like finely cut gems, their sparkle blinds us to the messy underground business of their procurement. Beginnings? Ha! They are not beginnings at all, only the point at which necessity dictates that the perpetrators let you in on the plot; otherwise, it's curtains.

Answer this: Is the throw of the dice not preceded by the unfolding of the table, the gathering of the players, the hedging of bets? The sublime first note of the symphony, does it not follow the painstaking tuning of the strings? And midnight's charms ... Who, in that heralding stroke filled with promise and new resolution, does not also give in to nostalgia and regret for the retreat of hopes unaccomplished?

Beginnings are for fools. By the time the new thing, the fresh start, the clean slate, whatever it is touted as, by the time it's put to you, it is already an old done deal from which you and I have been excluded, but for which, sooner or later, we will end up paying the price.

A few years ago I was passing through London when a friend invited me to a 'must-see' opera in a rundown East End music hall. I found it a disorienting and confusing experience, but was also so compelled by it that I returned the following night in the hope of a cancellation to see the show a second time.

There was nothing conventional about this production, so if conventional mythology is what you're after, feel free to exit now. Attempting to outline it sequentially here is to undermine one of its most remarkable features. It looped and wound and scrolled through time so that everything seemed to be happening at once, the past, having no concept of a safe following distance, colliding with the present, when things suddenly ground to a halt. For a start, there was no start, just a huge maelstrom of promising prospects intertwined with everything that had ever been, like old creepers twisting around new growth in a forest in spring. Beginnings banished, the audience was allowed into the auditorium only after the performance had already begun. There would be no orderly and contrived taking up of seats – deprived. There would be no relaxed browsing through the programme – rejected. Fuck curtain calls and polite applause for the bowing conductor and the tenor clearing his throat. All conventional expectations – denied.

Another striking thing about 'the beginning' was how cast members had infiltrated the unsuspecting audience as they milled around the foyer sipping drinks before the performance. A man who came up to me claiming to have recognised me turned out to be the president in the show.

'What a voice,' I marvelled when he sang his first 'Aria of Pardon', which moved me all the more because I felt as though I knew him or, more to the point, I felt as though he knew me.

Rather than the sedate and dignified tone we associate with opera, the effect of all of this was more akin to the marketplace, with people scrambling for position as some tried to stake claims to seats they still perceived as theirs and others waved arms in the air as they got separated from companions, watching helplessly as they got swept away by the crowd, leaving them to the daunting realisation that they would have to face the music on their own. Less Royal Opera House, more rush-hour commuter train, the journey doesn't commence when you step aboard or end when you disembark. And at the opera, just as in life, you have to make do as best you can with the space you find. And the president, however much you might feel that he is singing for you, well, in the end, like the rest of the cast, he also has a scripted part to play.

The props were simple, paying homage to the faded grandeur of the old music hall. At one end of the stage, a well-placed marble column positioned under an arch of the hall suggested the Roman Forum. Lit up in the centre of the stage, a wooden structure with doors open at both ends signified the temple of the Roman god of gods, knower of what is past and of what is yet to come, the chaos before formation, the embers after destruction – Janus, the two-faced Roman god of boundaries and thresholds, gates and doors, transitions and beginnings. The doors of the Temple of Janus stood open, a sign that Rome was at war. At the foot of the temple steps the town crier took to his platform while the audience was still in unseated chaos.

Recitative of the Town Crier

Good people of Rome, order yourselves. I bring news that soon the gates of the Temple of Janus will be closed, bringing an end to our long and bitter war with the enemies of the Republic. The closing of the Gates of War will be a new beginning and a time of new justice and new prosperity for all …

The First Darkness

The lights fade on the town crier, and on the temple and the stage and the auditorium, until there is only darkness. Having been preconditioned into expecting that theatrical darkness will pass, the audience waits for the light. But it does not come. Disconcerted, the audience members start murmuring to the strangers now seated randomly beside them.

The First Light

Just as their unnerving is about to climax, a single spotlight draws the audience's attention to a room suspended above the auditorium. An aide steps into the light.

Duet of the Aide and the President

Aide: *Sir, it's time.*

In a padded leather chair a man swings around. I immediately identify him as the man from the foyer who pretended to recognise me. I know that guy, I want to shout.

President: *I know.*

The president steps out onto a precarious ledge and looks down at the audience. In various locations around the auditorium, television screens flicker on, broadcasting this image of this man on a ledge.

Aria of the New Future

PRESIDENT: *Romans, we have gathered here in the Forum and across the Republic tonight to embark upon a new journey into a new future. That new future is just a few short minutes away. We implore Janus to preside over our new beginning and pray that he will find our libations worthy.*

The Second Darkness

Fade to darkness. Only the TV screens remain on. The audience watches the footage on the screens being rewound to a point in the past where three generals are seen entering the Forum escorted by heavily armed guards.

The Second Light

The generals enter the Forum under heavy guard. They ascend the staircase leading to the president's room above the auditorium. Sitting there in his padded leather chair is my friend, the president. The third general gestures towards the ledge. The president rises from his seat and steps out onto the ledge.

Quartet of the Generals and the President

Third General: *Your people await.*

Second General: *Eighty thousand gathered tonight. An impressive showing.*

President: *Generals are not allowed inside the pomerium, as well you know. Weapons are not allowed inside the pomerium, as well you know. We are all citizens here. To what do Romans owe this affront?*

First General: *To ensure that things proceed as they should. Omens are wont to reside in beginnings. Study the rooftops. Survey the crowds.*

Laser beams illuminate marksmen in the rafters and assassins in the crowd. This is a terrifying moment, and I begin to feel as though this whole crazy performance is in fact an act staged by psychotic killers intent on mowing us all down.

First General: *Whatever changes in the Republic tonight, this balance remains the same. Remember our agreement.*

The Third Darkness

Aware that we are now being held hostage, the third darkness is disconcerting. The woman next to me grabs hold of my hand the moment the lights go out. She does not release her grip, even when the television screens flicker back on, the footage looping forward to the period of The Third Light.

The Third Light

Duet of the Aide and the President – Cycle II

AIDE: *Sir, it's time.*

In a padded leather chair a man swings around. I am not excited when I recognise him this time. I am just a sucker who's been had.

PRESIDENT: *I know.*

The president steps out onto a precarious ledge and looks down at the audience. In various locations around the auditorium, television screens flicker on, broadcasting this image of this man on a ledge.

Aria of Pardon

PRESIDENT: *Romans, we have gathered here in the Forum and across the Republic tonight to embark upon a new journey into a new future. That future is just a few short minutes away. We implore Janus to preside over our new beginning and pray that he will find our libations worthy.*

'Biformed Janus, source of years gliding by in silence, who alone amongst the immortal celestials sees his own back, come, attend our nobles as Your guests, those whose labours secure delightful pastimes for the earth, and peace on earth, peace on the seas. Attend and bless Your senators and those of the people of Rome, the Quirites, and with a nod open Your gleaming gates onto peaceful precincts.'

Romans, we have gathered here in the Forum and across the Republic tonight to embark upon a new journey into a new future. That future is just a few short minutes away. We implore Janus to preside over our new beginning and pray that he will find our libations worthy.

But beginnings are begotten by endings and the future is the offspring of the past. Let us lay that past to rest.

I have heard the confessions of those generals who, during the course of the war, have inflicted grievous suffering on the people of Rome. Whatever the suffering, we must remember that they are honourable generals of Rome, who were carrying out their duties and orders in the service of the Republic.

The choice that faces the Republic in transition is retribution or reprieve.

Under the guidance of Janus we have chosen reprieve.

Through this act of grace we have laid the firmest cornerstone in the foundations of our new Republic.

Let the Gates of War be closed.

In the background, the doors of the Temple of Janus are drawn closed.

As the Gates of War are closed, marking the end of our long and bitter conflict, so let us lay down our swords. Rome is once again at peace, and let our first utterance on the threshold of the new era be 'Pardon'.

After the show, I hailed a cab. When it pulled up under the light of a street lamp, I noticed that it was not the standard black London cab. This one was painted in the colours of the new South African flag. Along the sides was emblazoned a very new kind of South African slogan: *South Africa. Now open for business.*

Of course I'm laughing. I'm laughing so loud I have tears streaming down my face. We've been had. Forget about beginnings. All we have is messy middles confused as twisted guts and eternal as the long intestine. From time to time, a new spin, new packaging and labels and faces to put on billboards, and new jargon to bandy about to show you're in the know. New, new, new, change, change, change, cheer, cheer, cheer.

No beginnings, just reinvented middles running on the loop. Like a never-ending soap, a couple of episodes and you're with the plot. Who cares how it started? Hell, who even remembers? The important thing is this: you're onto them. And you've seen enough to know that this week's beauty will be next week's beast …

You sorry sods. Shampoo, however they might try to reinvent it, is shampoo. Read the label. Like impacted guts, it's just the same old shovelling of the same old shit. But still, you fell for it, because you think you're worth it. And now you're standing there in your shower, with shit running down your face.

Fuck the word. In the beginning there was compromise.

*

For Archbishop Desmond Tutu, its most high-profile proponent, it was about 'forgiveness'. For the family of Steve Biko, its most high-profile critics, it was a 'vehicle for political expediency'. Coming up on Radio ANA after the news, Lucas Molope considers the legacy of South Africa's Truth and Reconciliation Commission …

This is Radio ANA in Dar es Salaam, Bamako, N'Djamena, Libreville and across Africa on TV, on radio and online.

Beep … The headlines at three o'clock ... Beep …

The BBC journalist Alan Johnston has been kidnapped in Gaza. Beep …

British soldiers accused of war crimes in Iraq evade justice. Beep …

Tibetan women commemorate Uprising Day in Dharamsala, India. Beep …

And Queen Elizabeth II delivers her annual broadcast as head of the Commonwealth. Beep …

With this and the rest of the news, here's Yasmin Shaheen. Beep …

Landau

In the old days they would sit on the stoep surveying the horizon, waiting. When they eventually caught sight of the dust cloud billowing along the rutted track that led up to the farmstead, they would rise, one by one – first his baby sister, jumping to her feet and shouting 'Landau!' before running out to meet him; then she, rising slowly, sighing slightly, pushing back her hair, tidying her apron; and finally his father, big as a house, stepping forward with the confident swagger of a man who is master of all he surveys. The day before he will have slaughtered an animal himself. Tonight it will be turning over the fire, a feast for all the families in the *omgewing* who will have gathered to celebrate the hero's return from the embattled border.

During the meal, Landau will limit himself to the 'pleasantries' of border operations – the camaraderie, the pranks, the jokes. After the meal, when the women will have made their retreat, taking the reluctant children with them, the men will lean forward thirstily over bottles of brandy to drink down the unabridged brutalities of war. She will watch him from the shadows, his fierce gesticulation silhouetted against the fire. Seeing him leap up to mime the pinning down of his enemy with booted foot, seeing him raise his right elbow into the air and aim an imaginary rifle downwards at the ground before the detailed re-enactment of the backward jolts that come with pulling the trigger again and again. Seeing his father noting proudly the faces around the fire filled with admiration and respect, she will conclude again that the anger her husband directed at his servants on the farm, her son aimed at men on the border.

The following morning she will be the first to rise, tiptoeing through the house and out into the garden, feeling compelled to retrieve her son from the simulated battlefield of drunken re-enactment before the servants catch sight of him by the burnt-out fire, slouched in a chair standing in a circle of empty chairs, a drained bottle cradled against his chest. She will haul him up, wishing that she could pull hard enough to release her son from the body of the soldier. Once he is on the bed she will remove his boots and unbutton his shirt. She will notice the dreadful new scar running down the length of his forearm, which the unseasonal long shirtsleeves will already have suggested to her. She will run a finger gently along its fresh, pink length. She can only speculate. He will never tell. For a while she will sit and watch him. Even in his stupor, he struggles, kicking and twitching. A thought will arise, but she will try to suppress it, unsuccessfully. It will linger, hanging in the air, mingling with the fumes of stale alcohol – hunting men is taking its toll.

'Those were the days,' reminisce her dwindling circle of farm friends, the days before her husband, Groot Landau, owner of the largest farm in the *omgewing*

and arch-strategist behind their own 'system of defence', keeled over just before he'd reached the high point of yet another zealous speech. She knew the climax was coming because she'd seen him rehearse it so many times, most recently in their bedroom that morning, dressed in a pair of Y-fronts made redundant by the overhang of another of his assets, which she reckoned to be the most expansive in the district, a bulging paunch. In anticipation of the climax in which he delivered his words deliberately, in a one-by-one staccato while simultaneously pounding a fat fist on a trembling podium, she saw him pause for effect and pull a handkerchief across his brow, a dramatic gesture, she supposed, contrived to convey a man ready to pour every last drop of blood, sweat and tears into the fulfilment of his convictions: 'This is our country. This is our land.'

Groot Landau had spoken. His audience exploded into convulsions of applause. Thinking it an impromptu addition to the script, she squirmed inwardly when he stepped out from behind the podium and fell to his knees, hand on heart, like a balding rock star on a comeback tour for diehard fans. But the crowd loved it, the sight of Groot Landau like a knight on bended knee pledging support before rising to lead them to victory, elevating them to yet further levels of exaltation. They stamped feet, banged chairs, clapped hands, blew horns, lifted clamouring children onto burly shoulders and unravelled flags usually displayed only in secret convocations. As their gallant knight sustained his chivalrous pose, their adulation grew louder, prompting the chorus master to run to the front, arms flailing wildly, hollering the refrain from a patriotic favourite, while on the stage behind him, Groot Landau fell forward flat on his face, legs twitching like stricken prey, leaving the enthusiastic singer, his back to the stage, to conduct a bewildered audience, while he continued in lone but full-throated voice to bellow: 'We will pledge to live or perish for our land and victory.'

'Yes, those were they days,' they sigh, sitting long-faced in a sorry circle in her living room. But she says nothing.

When they rise to leave – 'It's getting late. Can't be too safe, these days, you know' – she thanks them for coming, only nodding in response to their invitations to visit.

'Perhaps it's still too soon,' one of them condescends before proceeding to pour po-faced pity on her.

'Still too many painful memories, I expect.'

She remains silent, knowing it will reassure their expectation that she be a mourning widow nurturing grief until her own end. Only her eternal misery will keep them happy.

The border she thought, had always thought, a brutal place that had sucked her son into a futile cause. She thought this so often that the words rearrange themselves into new permutations in her head, like when she used to sit at the kitchen table staring at the radio for so long that it no longer resembled a radio but rather some unfathomable thing from which came strange unfathomable sounds: the border, a futile place that sucked in my futile son; the place, a futile border that sucked in my brutal son. Whatever the mutation, she never expressed it aloud. Life was troubled enough and she lonely enough not to risk further isolation. So she did nothing and waited for futility to run its course. Nothing could prevent the inevitable. The border, a brutal place that sucked my cruel son into a futile cause. Yet some desperate part of her still wanted to redeem him; the border, a compulsory place that sucked in my dutiful son. That must count for something. It won him medals.

Somewhere

They say that if you stay in one place long enough you'll eventually see someone you know. They lied. These vacant walls are filled only with fear. And longing. To capture and to show. Those have been my pursuits. To strive constantly against the dark clouds, which threaten to engulf and overcome the uninformed mind. Now, all I know with certainty is that I have come to know nothing. All my affirmations negated. That is terrifying.

I don't know where I am. I don't know how long I've been here. I don't know who my keepers are. I don't know why I'm being kept. I don't know what they think I've done. Or might do. And after all this time alone, the clouds are closing in and I'm no longer sure of myself. Has that been their project?

How long has it been? When do minutes gather into hours and hours amass into days? When does the brightness of daylight surrender to the quiet subtlety of night? These walls have no answers.

The food in the hatch, is it breakfast, lunch or dinner? Always the same unvarying rice and beans, as consistent as my isolation, as devoid of distinguishing feature as the blank walls that enclose me. Do these bland meals arrive at regular intervals? Would three mark a day? Sometimes I am famished, devouring anonymity. Sometimes I am not.

Deprived of references, I look to my body as a measure of time, the growth of my stubble, the length of my nails. But how reliable a measure of time is the male body? A woman would know a month.

How long do habits take to break? They say two weeks. I always used to wake with the first light of dawn filtering through the curtains. So when did I start to sleep in this constant fluorescent light? I have nothing against which to mark the change, not an hour, not a day. Stripped. Totally. The imprint of my wristwatch, the crescent of thickened skin at the base of my ring finger, they too have abandoned me. How silently, like the moon receding, have my life's footprints waned from my body.

Out of reach on the ceiling is a smoke alarm. With what would I start a fire? It has a tiny red light, which flashes once every three seconds. One, two, three, flash … one, two, three, flash … How many flashes in a minute? I sit up with renewed vigour to grapple with the calculation, making sums on the floor with my finger. Twenty. How many in an hour? One thousand two hundred. Yes! I have overcome. I have found a measure.

So I start to count. One, two, three, flash … one, two, three, flash …

One, two, three, flash … But, one, two, three, flash … hope, one, two, three, flash … quickly, one, two, three, flash … starts, one, two, three, flash … to, one, two, three, flash … fade, one, two, three, flash …

I can never turn away from the flashing light. It will be the centre of my new contracted universe. Like an abandoned telescope angled at some distant planet,

I will always be focused on the flashing light. I will swap the ramblings of my idle mind for the discipline of counting. Random words for ordered numbers. I consider the choice ... With stamina I could estimate twenty-four hours. I would have to count one, two, three, flash ... four, five, six, flash ... seven, eight nine, flash ... all the way to twenty-eight thousand eight hundred. Could I sustain that? What would be my reward, my sense of achievement, at the end of such a day? The king was in his counting house counting all his money.

In desperation I turn to base bodily function, counting the times I crouch over the stained bucket that appears in alternating cycles in the same hatch as the rice and beans. Rice and beans ... stinky-linky bucket ... one, two, three, flash ... rice and beans ... stinky-linky bucket ... one, two, three, flash ... I have squatted sixty-three times since counting began. How compelled a man feels to record his days. If a squat is a day ... I am struck by a realisation. I have decoded their design. My jaw drops. I stand up and hold my head in my hands. I have been defeated. My life is most measurable in buckets of shit.

And why withhold the longing when I have admitted to the fear? Longing, tick, fear ... fear, tock, longing ... The agonising counterpoints, which rock the pendulum of my tormented mind. I long for Leila. I long to see her face. Again and again I close my eyes to summon her, but just as she takes shape, her eyes meeting mine, fear and longing snatch her away. Falling to my knees, eyes screwed tightly shut against the light, I pound my fists on the concrete floor, willing her back. Leila? Leila! But it's no use. She is gone. Imprisonment has stripped her ring from my finger; now isolation, picking at my brain like a vulture at a carcass, is eroding her face from my mind. How much longer before there is nothing? Before I am completely hollowed out, like the echoing chambers of a long-deserted city.

I long for Leila. Leila's sound, Leila's smell, Leila's laugh, Leila's touch. I long for Leila hovering over me in her preferred way, her dark hair bouncing in thick trusses around her shoulders, my hands cupped around her breasts, rubbing down her sides, moving over her hips and down to her legs until our bodies convulse in a rhythm all of their own.

Leila once recorded an interview I gave on TV.

'See,' she would say, freezing a frame. 'That smile there. You should smile it more often.'

I found it difficult to know what Leila thought of my work, but I sensed then that she might have been proud.

But look, Leila, look at me now, grovelling for you on a dirty prison mattress, howling for you like a madman. What would you think of me now, Leila, now that the hourglass of my immeasurable confinement drips with buckets of shit and loads of self-induced cum?

Spent, I clutch my thin pillow and curl crying into sleep. Leila? Leila! Do you know where I am? Are you searching to find me? Have you forgotten me, Leila?

Leila, do you long for me too?

But Leila never answers. That makes the longing worse.

And the fear.

Have they taken Leila too?

THE NEWS AT NOON

This is ANA in Asmara, Juba, Cotonou, Accra and across Africa on TV, on radio and online.

Desperate Measures *was presented by Angela Frasier and produced by Norman Cole. It was a Rough & Ready production for ANA. If you have been affected by any of the issues raised in the programme, please contact us by email at desperatemeasures@radioana.com ... In a couple of minutes, we'll have the news at midday, but before then, here's Jacob Moma with a look ahead at this week's* Reading Out Loud ...

Good morning, readers. Regular listeners to our show will be familiar with Rida Osman, who first appeared on the programme last year when his story 'Cola Pistol' won our Write to Life short story competition. Well, last month saw the publication of Osman's first novel, *Writing Notes*, the quirky tale of a lonely young adolescent who tries to discover the truth behind his best friend's apparent suicide in a slum where 'gossips in curlers camped out permanently on street corners like five-dollar whores on a Saturday night'. *Writing Notes* is the focus of this week's *Reading Out Loud*. Does gossip plus gossip make truth? To find out, join me, Jacob Moma, for *Reading Out Loud*, every day at twelve fifteen, after the midday news.

*

Beep ... This is Radio ANA, with the headlines at noon. Beep ...

Leila Mashal, the wife of captured photojournalist Tariq Hassan, has been placed under house arrest in South Africa. Beep ...

In war-ravaged Kasalia, rebel troops have taken the country's second-largest city, Wana'a, on the same day as three mortar bombs rock the capital, Kas. Beep ...

And demonstrations continue in the Tunisian capital of Tunis, after a street vendor sets himself alight in protest against municipal harassment. Beep ...

With this and the rest of the news, here's Rebecca Richardson. Beep ...

*

Good afternoon. In an unprecedented development, Dr Leila Mashal, the wife of captured photojournalist Tariq Hassan, has been placed under house arrest in Johannesburg by South Africa's largest private security firm, ZARCorps. Her incarceration, seven months after her husband's abduction from a Johannesburg hotel, comes in the wake of the recent barrage of accusations regarding the South African government's close dealings with ZARCorps. Her detention has led to protests at South African high commissions and embassies around the world. Dr Mashal has herself been an increasingly vocal critic of private military and security companies in her campaign as an independent candidate in the upcoming municipal elections.

Governments around the world have condemned these developments, and in a joint statement, international human rights groups, democracy campaigners and trade union movements criticised ZARCorps' actions as 'the most alarming manifestation to date of the corporate security coup currently under way in South Africa'. Neither the South African government nor ZARCorps were available for comment. Our correspondent Suleiman Muso filed this report from Johannesburg …

Leila Mashal's life as a medical doctor took a dramatic turn seven months ago when her husband, Tariq Hassan, was abducted in Johannesburg. Since then, she has become increasingly vocal in her criticism of the South African government's association with big business, in particular, private military and security firms. Last night she launched her campaign in Johannesburg as an independent candidate for the municipal elections. In her inaugural campaign speech delivered at the University of the Witwatersrand, she spoke about the issue of freedom, warning a packed auditorium of the dangers behind the proliferation of undemocratic force:

'While South Africans hold the vote, they don't hold the power. Our constitutional structures are being hollowed out, withholding power from the electorate and their elected officials and concentrating it in the grip of a secret and unaccountable cabal of oligarchs whose names and faces the electorate will never know.'

She concluded her speech with the following words: 'Freedom? Tariq is not free. I am not free. There is no freedom. There is only the fight for freedom.'

Her words proved prophetic. While the details of her detention remain unclear, it appears that Dr Mashal was prevented from leaving her home for the airport earlier this morning, when heavily armed ZARCorps security personnel laid siege to her property, confiscating cellphones and computer equipment. We have been told that telephone lines to the property have also been cut.

ZARCorps was not available for comment. The corporation provides security for foreign embassies, major financial institutions and mineral and oil fields in almost all of the world's major conflict zones. It appears that at the time of his abduction, Tariq Hassan had been investigating darker accusations that ZARCorps security personnel as well as government officials were complicit in corruption, extortion, kidnapping, torture, destabilisation and targeted assassinations in Kasalia. In an interview with this network just hours before his abduction, Tariq Hassan estimated ZARCorps' revenues from the conflict in Kasalia alone to be in the region of $300 million.

Dr Mashal had been due to speak at the University of the Western Cape in Cape Town tonight, an appearance which has now been cancelled.

Thank you, Suleiman. Now, as we've heard, Leila Mashal had been due to speak at the University of the Western Cape, but despite the cancellation of her appearance, huge crowds have continued to gather at the university during the course of the afternoon as news of her detention spreads. Let's cross over to

Cape Town now. Our reporter Khadija Adams is at UWC. Khadija, bring us up to date with what's been happening down there …

Somewhere

I used to speak in tongues of four and dream only in one. But now I dream in tongues of four and speak only in none. Is it today? It feels like yesterday.

Darkness. How delicious it would be if somebody turned out the light for half an hour. Fifteen minutes. Even five would be a relief. But all I have is brightness and thoughts and all I can do is watch them line up in my head, readying themselves to replay over and over again, like a nightmare on a loop, becoming stronger with every repetition, more emboldened, fitter still to repeat, to repeat, to repeat …

Sometimes in the midst of the repetition, a new thought flickers. The novelty excites me, like a splash of colour in a black and white world. There might even be something in it, I hope, the outline of a new project, perhaps an article, who knows, perhaps even a book. But no sooner has the new thought flashed than I immediately start to fear for its safety, realising that I have no way of protecting it, of recording it, of hiding it in safe keeping from all the other repetitive devouring thoughts that hang around like gangsters in the seething ghettoes of my mind, protecting their patch against would-be invaders.

Still, I can't give up just like that. I must persevere.

I bolster my new idea, blowing desperately on its embers so that it will burst into flame and illuminate my mind with newness and novelty. I encourage the sparks, coax them, nurture them, expand a little here, give a little more there.

Yes, they're coming on nicely now, a gentle glow of fresh innovation starting to take shape. Watching it form, wanting to encourage it to the next level of originality, I begin to realise why I wonder so obsessively about time, because how does one develop thoughts when they can't be arranged into a reliable sequence? How do I determine progression if I cannot say: Yesterday I thought such-and-such, which leads me towards thinking so-and-so today? For when was 'yesterday'? And when is 'today', when my only measuring devices are four blank walls, which keep my body ever stranded but tug so constantly at my mind that I fear it will be dislodged from its mooring and sent hopelessly afloat and I would not even be able to tell the day it happened.

These white walls force me down and deeper down into the abyss of my mind. One needs pressurised vessels to go that deep and a depressurisation chamber upon resurfacing. The bright light bounces off them like flashing blades so that I have to close my eyes to spare them the pain. But closing my eyes eases one kind of pain while initiating another. With closed eyes, the nightmare on the loop starts to roll again. Open eyes, blinding walls; closed eyes, nightmares.

I've confessed to fear and longing, but is there anything else lurking in the depths? I must shut it out. Figments of the darkness. But the feeling persists, until it threatens to overwhelm, like when you're out of your depth and running out of breath, hoping you have time to make it to the surface, limbs flailing desperately against the pressure holding you back, keeping you down. That thing holding you down has a name. It's called shame and this is how it works: it holds you down by shutting your mouth and tormenting your brain.

I've resumed counting. I've worked out a way. I partially cup my hands around my eyes like shields from the sharpness of the light, then I count. One, two three, flash ... one, two, three, flash ... I've reached three thousand. Not in one sitting, that would be too tedious. These days I'm content with counting as long as I can. Usually I get to one hundred and fifty before I've had enough. Then I repeat 150, 150, 150, so that I will remember to start from 150 the next time I count. Counting is easier than confronting shame.

And then there's work. Yes, I'm intending a new book. I've already got an outline of chapters roughly figured out. Roughly is all I can manage under the circumstances because I can't get my thoughts to form a neat line and stand still. To seize control of my project I would need pen and paper to keep the letters and the words and the sentences and the paragraphs in check. But I'm alone and they're taking me for granted, plotting a mutiny on my ship. They jump around like unruly children on a poorly supervised school trip, bouncing on the seats of the school bus, throwing around the contents of their packed lunches, touching the exhibits in the museum until the teachers just give up and let the chaos reign.

But I will not be defeated. I have an idea. The wall

at my feet will be chapter one, the wall to my right will be chapter two, at my head is chapter three, to my left is chapter four, the ceiling five, the floor six. I move my hands across the walls as I write, the words forming under my fingers as I move them across the blank writing surface. I'm a little concerned about what I'll do when I've used up all the wall space, because I envisage more than six chapters. What will I do when I've used up every surface in the room and written myself into that corner over there? How will I continue once I've run out of space, when my chapters start to push into one another like tectonic plates, Afghanistan colliding with Kasalia, Afghanistan and Kasalia crashing into Palestine, Afghanistan and Kasalia and Palestine merging with Darfur? I wouldn't just be able to wipe the walls clean like a whiteboard without a permanent record of my six chapters. And if I've written myself into a corner, how would I ever be able to get out? I couldn't just walk across the floor, smudging my writing with size thirteen footprints.

This is ANA in Cairo, Lusaka, Pretoria, Maputo and across Africa on TV, on radio and online.

Last week, Herman Wallace and Albert Woodfox observed a very bleak anniversary. Both men, now in their sixties, have been held in solitary confinement in Louisiana State Prison for forty years.

What are the effects of long-term isolation on the body and the mind? Why is it used? Should it be classified as a form of torture and outlawed?

Join Ashraf Sadiqi as he investigates solitary confinement. That's Ashraf Sadiqi, presenting Alone *here on ANA at eleven o'clock this morning, just after the news.*

PART III

I hurt myself today
To see if I still feel
I focus on the pain
The only thing that's real

– Johnny Cash

Reading Out Loud

This is ANA in Rabat, Freetown, Tunis, Lilongwe and across Africa on TV, on radio and online.

Next on ANA is Jacob Moma with this week's edition of Reading Out Loud. *But first we take a look ahead at a new series starting soon on Radio ANA,* The Silent Coup: Who Holds the Power?

South Africa, 1994. It was a time for euphoria. South Africans watched in awe as pop stars and world leaders lined up to shake hands with their new president. A year later, they painted their faces with the colours of their country's new flag to celebrate the Rugby World Cup.

But what was really going on? Why, exactly, were British, French, German, Italian, and Swedish politicians and executives from European arms manufacturers like French Thale and British BAE forming queues to meet the president?

Because the newly elected South African government was about to make its largest post-apartheid purchase – estimated to be in excess of R30 billion – of weapons to modernise its military arsenal.

Yet, with no clear foreign military threat to South Africa and despite the insistence of civil society leaders that the country's financial resources would be better spent on education, health and housing, the government pressed ahead with the purchase.

Despite repeated attempts by the government to bury the scandal, allegations of corruption and multimillion dollar bribes to ANC leaders and politicians by companies such as BAE have never gone away.

In South Africa the government has recently announced the reopening of an inquiry into the now notorious arms deal.

Why now? Is the inquiry a cover-up in which a few symbolic heads will roll for the cameras while a deeper, more sinister truth remains secret? Was the arms deal in fact a new kind of coup in which power was silently seized from the electorate while they were out celebrating a hollow election victory and a sham transfer to democracy?

In a new series of programmes, ANA tries to uncover the nature of real power in post-apartheid South Africa and who really controls it. That's The Silent Coup: Who Holds The Power?, *coming soon on Radio ANA.*

But now, it's over to Jacob Moma, host of Reading Out Loud.

PRESENTER: Good afternoon, readers. This is Jacob Moma welcoming you to another edition of *Reading Out Loud*. My special guest today was the winner of last year's Write to Life competition for his story 'Cola Pistol'. Well, I'm pleased to say that Rida Osman is back with us, this time with a new novel called *Writing Notes*. Welcome, Rida.

Rida: Thank you, Jacob.

Presenter: Also in the studio with us is a panel of readers whose names have, as usual, been drawn from a hat. They've come along to ask Rida questions about his writing and his new novel. Welcome to you all as well. But before we get to questions from the panel, I'd like to start with you, Rida. You're going to be reading an extract from the novel in a few minutes, but before you do so, I wonder if you could just set the scene a bit for our listeners by telling us a little about this story. It's a murder mystery, I believe, or should I say a suicide mystery?

Rida: It is. The story is about an awkward teenager whose insecurities stem from having been disfigured by an arson attack on his home. But with his injuries comes a new intuition, a kind of sixth sense, so that when his best friend is found dead, he suspects it's not the suicide it's portrayed to be. A budding ventriloquist, the teenager has only one confidant: a puppet named Vocal. I'll be reading from the title chapter fairly early on in the book.

~Writing Notes~

We're on our rooftop, me and Vocal, watching the sun rise over our neighbourhood.

'Neighbourhood?' Vocal contests. 'Are you trying to mislead your audience?'

I know Vocal. He'll answer his own question, so I say nothing.

'"Neighbourhood" conjures images of trees and lawns and nuclear families with cars and double garages and who live in houses that stand separate from one another.'

I see Vocal's point as I survey our tumbledown surroundings: the lopsided buildings straining under the weight of giant water tanks, shaded by the brims of wide satellite dishes, and stumbling up and down the crooked streets like a multitude of drunken amigos under sombreros pushing ungainly barrels up a hill.

I look at Vocal, who has a wide-eyed, enthusiastic expression constantly etched on his face. Even when we are hungry and broke, which is often the case, even when the news is bad, which it always seems to be, even when absolutely everybody is exhausted by absolutely everything, I can still rely on good old Vocal always looking keen. He turns to look at me.

'You should get going,' he says.

'Where to?' I ask.

Vocal beckons me closer. I move my right ear up to his mouth.

'To school,' he says.

So, here I am again, one of thirty-nine, writing notes. I used to be one of forty-one, but that was before Abigail Cloete had to be withdrawn from school because she fell pregnant from Sol Josephs – Sol – whose father called him Suleiman and whose mother called him Solomon, but whom we all called Sol.

To be true, there are as many versions of Sol's final hours as there are tongues construing them, but this is what I came across in the mist during an early morning walk while tongues were still asleep.

Judge for yourself: Sol's father's blue Datsun parked under a tree on the side of a dirt track on the outskirts of town, a hosepipe leading from the exhaust into the right rear window, the cabin smoky as a clubhouse, Sol stretched out in the reclined driver's seat pushed all the way back from the steering wheel, a half-drunk bottle of JD in his stiffened fist, a few smoked-out joints in the ashtray and, in the tape deck, 'Hotel California' playing on the loop.

Apparently, his mother is supposed to have told the police how she'd heard Sol recording the song over and over again the previous afternoon. Some say that was when she shed her first tears, during her statement to the police. They say it was sorrow inflicted by guilt. A neighbour who claims to have been present in the house, having tea and peanut butter sandwiches with his mother at the kitchen table during Sol's recording session, apparently heard his mother prophesy with scorn: 'Yesterday it was a madrassa in Karachi. Today it's a hotel in California. Tomorrow it will be a padded cell in the bloody madhouse if you carry on like this.'

According to the cousin of the brother-in-law of somebody who was at school with a sister of one of the investigating officers, Sol had not used a blank cassette to record his chosen swansong, but one on which his father had originally recorded a special tribute to Nusrat Fateh Ali Khan from Basmati FM. As a result of the overlay, Sol's repeated recordings of 'Hotel California' were interspersed with throwbacks to Nusrat's underlying mystical Sufi qawwalis and intermittent jingles from the host radio station, so that Sol's tape sounded something like this:

You can check in any time you like
But you can never leave
Glitch
Shamas-Ud-Doha
Badar-Ud-Doja
Jhoole Jhoole Lal
Glitch
They sharpen all their steely knives
But they just can't kill the beast
Glitch
Basmati FM
The Rice of Life

But who knows? Does gossip plus gossip make truth? In this neighbourhood – Vocal and I have not yet agreed on a suitable alternative designation – nothing usurps a tragedy like malice, and throughout that time gossips in curlers camped out permanently on street corners like five-dollar whores on a Saturday night.

About the funeral, they speculated, from the church or from the mosque? Condolences and announcements, would they be published in the newspaper or would word be left to spread? His position in the grave, they wondered, on his back or on his side? But above all, above all else, their deliberations centred on this – would *she* be there, staring down into the adolescent grave into which her wicked accusation had condemned him? How quickly her proper name of three syllables had been devoured by an impersonal pronoun of one. Gossip eats names.

All that may well be, but this is what I know: everybody called Sol a friend, but he only had one – me. Odd, mutilated, balaclava-wearing, puppet-talking me, and this is what I know – Sol hated JD. He wouldn't touch the stuff, not since we got violently ill from it after a stint of teenage bingeing on our rooftop a few months before my 'accident'. The only way Sol would have drunk half a bottle of JD is if he'd had it poured down his throat.

I went to visit Abigail during one of those evenings when the atmosphere was rancid with rumour, my visit prompted by the realisation that it was a liberty only I was free to take; conventional people, I figured, expect odd things from odd people.

Shame, I heard them whisper as I passed by.

Of all the people to discover a body ...

Could push him further over the edge, you know.

I opened the gate and walked up the path to the front step. I stood on the mat that said 'Welcome' and rang the doorbell. It plays a famous tune. I recognised it. It goes *la la la la la la la la la*. The tune continued to play until Abigail's brother opened the door. I was not expecting him. He was older than me and a prestigious scholarship had taken him to a university far away. I supposed it was all this stuff with Abigail and Sol that must have brought him back. I greeted him, but he, registering only my balaclava, said nothing.

'Who is it, Alexander?' I heard a woman's voice call from inside the house.

Alex. Alex Cloete. He was the head boy at our school two years ago.

'I'm not sure,' he replied. 'I think it's the police.'

Alex must not have heard about the fire.

'The police?' The woman's voice sounded vexed. 'Well, invite them in. I'm coming.'

They had such confident strides, Alex and his deputies, like princes prancing through colonnades. How the juniors used to sidestep whenever they approached.

'No, I'm not the —,' I was going to explain, but Alex pulled the door wide open and gestured me in.

'I'm not —,' I tried again, but no sooner had I stepped through the door than Alex disappeared into the recesses of the house, from where I could hear him whispering urgently to his mother.

Even though I could only hear the consonants, '... th ... s ... sp ... g ...', context and instinct allowed me to fill the gaps – 'I think it's a special agent'.

Mrs Cloete stopped suddenly when she entered the room.

'Oh, it's you!' she said, and then she smiled, looking instantly more relaxed. 'Alexander told me it was the police. He doesn't know about the ... you know ...' She hesitated, nodding at my face while waving her hand in circles around hers.

'That's okay, Mrs Cloete,' I reassured her. Then I stated the reason for my visit. 'I've come to see Abigail.'

My eyes were drawn to the movement of a figure hovering out of view. Mrs Cloete registered it too.

'Abigail's not here now,' she said. 'But I'll tell her you came to visit.'

I reached into my pocket. 'I've brought her something,' I said, handing over my gift. And then that strange new feeling came over me, which forces me to forget about ceremony and to make for the nearest exit without saying goodbye.

When it came to it, I could not enter the graveyard. At the gates, I slipped away from the mourners while a flank of men drew Sol from the back of the purring hearse and lifted him to their shoulders. I watched as the cortège processed deeper and deeper into the garden of death, with Sol held shoulder high. When they all disappeared amongst the grey tombstones, which rose like a stunted skyline against the horizon, I sat down on the pavement and looked down at my school shoes.

It was while I was staring at my scuffed shoes outside the graveyard, where somewhere deep inside Sol was being lowered into his grave – Sol, the class joker; Sol, who placed stink bombs and itching powder on teachers' chairs; Sol, whose habitual and dishevelled late appearance at school inspired in all of us the hope that, yes, in this dull and dreary day, there might still be some fun to be had; Sol, whose legendary collection of porn magazines he would flash samples of in the boys' toilets in exchange for homework favours; Sol, my one and only protector, who once thrashed a bully who tried to remove my balaclava – it was then, while I was staring at my shoes and while Sol was being covered with earth, that somebody came to sit quietly on the pavement next to me.

I looked up. It was Abigail. She was not in her school uniform. In her hand she clutched one of the embroidered handkerchiefs I'd left with her mother. It was a set of three, one blue, one yellow and one pink. I'd found it amongst my mother's things that survived the fire. Abigail was holding the blue one. She looked at me, a tear running down her cheek.

'It's a lie,' she said. 'I'm not pregnant.'

'I know,' I said. 'And Sol didn't drink JD.'

Across the road, a car door opened. It was Alex. Abigail took her cue. She put the handkerchief to her cheek and wiped away her tears.

She crossed the road. I stood up. She got into the car. Alex shut the door. He looked at me. He got into the car. They drove away.

After the funeral I stayed on the bus beyond the last stop, all the way to the depot, just the driver and me. In town I walked the streets. In one street I had to sidestep a group of labourers who were sealing off a fresh stretch of pavement with bright orange plastic netting. In the gaming arcade I broke my previous record in one go. But I did not feel victorious. I left my bonus game for a group of kids who had gathered round to watch my remarkable achievement. They fought over the joysticks as I walked away.

In the empty music section of a large department store I tinkered on a keyboard.

'Do you play?' a sales assistant asked me.

'No,' I said, searching for the tune.

'Not bad for a beginner,' the sales assistant said with a smile when I'd pieced the *la la* tune together.

'What's it called?' I asked the assistant.

'That's Beethoven. "Für Elise". Would you like the sheet music? We've got a copy on the shelves.'

Again that strange feeling came over me, but being in a posh department store and because this man had been kind, I wrestled with the strangeness, forced a courteous 'No, thank you' and walked away.

A few steps into my departure, I sensed the man's puzzlement. I felt I owed him an explanation after he had been so kind. I stopped. I turned around.

'I don't have a piano,' I said. And then I turned to leave.

'You mean you've never played that piece before?' I heard the man ask behind me.

I stopped but did not turn around to face him.

'No,' I said. 'But it's been circling my mind. I wanted to know what it was called.' I continued towards the exit.

'I give lessons. I can teach you,' the man said.

I was feeling very awkward now, so I acknowledged the offer with a nod but rushed towards the door.

I walked to the fresh slab of pavement. The labourers had left. I picked out a match from the gutter and scratched three letters in the concrete – SOL.

The next time I was in town I walked to that pavement. My three letters had been adapted. Someone had prefixed them with an 'A' and an 'S'. Between my 'S' and my 'O' they had squeezed in an 'H' and after my 'L' they had added an 'E'. There was nothing I could do. The concrete had dried, leaving the word 'ASSHOLE' set in stone.

Mail Delivery System

I dine on past nights out. I draw long baths and lie in them for hours. I'd swim, were it not for my audience of armed men who emerge from their lairs around the property whenever I step outside the house. I burn frankincense from Somalia and slip under the bubbles.

Outside the bathroom window grows a bougainvillea, taking up the full view from the window. Tariq planted it there, knowing it to be my favourite plant and the bath my favourite place. But it is only in partial view now. I keep the blind down against the prying eyes so that it hangs just above the ledge, revealing only a slither of bougainvillea.

I dip below the water, where I hang suspended in a swirl of memories. When the lift doors opened, there was Yahya, waiting in the foyer. When we had greeted and exchanged pleasantries, he gestured towards the door.

'Shall we?'

It was only when we stepped out onto the pavement and Yahya had to extricate his arm in order to hail a taxi, that I realised I had hooked my arm in his while we crossed the foyer. It had been a spontaneous gesture on my part, and one of which Yahya had made no fuss. I knew then that we would be friends.

'I thought we were walking,' I said when the taxi pulled up.

Yahya looked down at my shoes. 'I don't think those were designed for Cairo streets.'

He sat in the front, chatting with the driver. I rode in the back, looking out at the city. When we arrived, an animated exchange erupted between Yahya and the driver. They were haggling over the fare, that much I could tell, but there was also something else going on. The driver said something that had clearly upset Yahya. I could see the anger on his face, but he did not respond. He simply put the money on the dashboard, stepped out of the taxi and opened the door for me at the back.

We entered the pub. It was quiet but would get very busy later on, Yahya explained. He guided me to a table, but did not sit down. He was still clearly agitated by the exchange with the taxi driver.

'What will you have to drink?' he asked when I was seated.

'Red wine, please.'

I watched him walk over to the bar, where he was greeted enthusiastically by a rotund man perched on a bar stool and by the barman, who was shining glasses. At one point, the barman pointed in my direction, and they all turned to look at me. I guessed they were curious and that Yahya was explaining who I was. I smiled and waved when they placed their hands on their hearts to acknowledge me.

Yahya returned to the table with a bottle and two glasses.

'Courtesy of Salem, the man on the stool,' he explained as he sat down. 'He's the owner. They know Tariq. He took that photo on the wall over there of

Salem and his wife, Susan. I guess she'll be in a bit later.'

When I looked over to locate the photograph, Salem raised his glass at me.

'Thank you,' I said, pointing at the wine.

'It's Egyptian,' Yahya said, pouring me a glass. 'I thought we'd go local.'

I studied the label, which read 'Omar Khayyám', before taking a sip.

'Okay?' Yahya asked, seeming concerned.

'It's fine,' I said and took another sip.

'That's good. You never know. It can be a bit inconsistent. Some bottles are fine but others can be like vinegar.'

He poured himself a glass and lit a cigarette.

A few awkward moments passed before I broke the silence.

'It's a lovely place.'

'It is. And Salem and his wife are good people. Tariq likes it too. We always end up here on the nights that he's in town. Have you heard from him today? How's he doing?

'We spoke briefly this morning. He seemed fine.'

Yahya nodded his head and moved around in his chair. I looked around the pub, although the word 'pub' was not descriptive. Back home it would qualify as a small boutique wine bar. It was cosy; the decor was of good taste; and from what I could tell of the few people dotted around, the clientele seemed rather well-to-do. We sat in an enclave surrounded by intricate screens.

'They're called *mashrabiya*,' Yahya explained. 'You can still see them on the windows of houses in the old city. The idea is that the women of the house could look out onto the street without anyone looking at them – they could see without being seen.'

But there was something mechanical about his explanation and Yahya seemed distracted, not fully present. I wanted to avoid more awkwardness, so I proceeded cautiously.

'I'm sorry if it's not my business, but what happened with the taxi driver? You seemed to be getting on so well.'

The incident in the taxi was clearly what had been distracting him, because Yahya didn't seem surprised by the question. Neither did he dismiss it.

'What an idiot guy,' he said shaking his head. 'He seemed fine, until it came to paying.'

'So he wanted more?'

'Much more, when I had already been quite generous. You know how it goes. He picked us up outside your hotel, you are clearly foreign, we were coming here, so you expect to pay a bit more, but he was being excessive.'

Yahya fell silent and took to swirling his wine around in his glass. But I sensed that there was more, so I persisted.

'So it was only an altercation about the fare?'

When Yahya looked up at me, I held his gaze.

'When I refused to pay what he demanded, he insulted me. He called me a cheap Palestinian. He said that Gaddafi was right to kick us out and that Egypt was right to keep us out. He said that if Mubarak let us in, we would come here and abuse the hospitality of Egyptians just as I was doing by not paying him the proper fare.'

Yahya drained his glass and lit another cigarette.

By persisting, I had opened a subject about which

I knew almost nothing. I would have assumed, if I even thought about it, that Arab support for the Palestinians would have been unanimous. So I drained my glass too and pushed it towards him for refilling.

'How did he know you were Palestinian?' Once asked, it seemed like a stupid question, but it was all I could think of asking.

'My accent.'

In just two words, Yahya's answer made me realise even more how limited my life had been, how much there was to learn. I had witnessed the exchange in Arabic between him and driver, but the distinguishing feature that had singled out Yahya for abuse had been totally lost on me. Another question sprang to mind. I did not speculate too much about its level of sophistication. If I did not ask, I would never learn.

'And do you think Gaddafi is right?'

'Gaddafi is mad. Why has he kicked out the Palestinians? To make a point about Israel? You humiliate the victims in order to make a point about the perpetrators?'

But Yahya had misunderstood my question. 'I didn't mean about ousting the Palestinians. I meant about Oslo. Is Gaddafi right about it being a farce?'

'Oh, that.' Yahya sighed. 'Let me tell you a joke.'

It was not the response I had been expecting, but it made me feel a little more relaxed, so I leaned forward to listen.

'The world had ended,' Yahya began, 'and all the nations of the earth had been sent either to heaven or to hell, all except the Palestinians. They were left standing alone in the square. When God got up from his throne to leave, the Palestinians called out, "What about us?"

'God turned around and asked, "Who are you?"

'The Palestinians replied, "We are the Palestinians."

'God sighed, "Oh, you lot."

'Then he turned to one of his angels and said, "Build them a refugee camp." '

I didn't know enough about the issues so I smiled, but Yahya laughed out loud.

'Of course Oslo is a joke. For my part, I've lived in so many places I can barely keep track. My father even more so. Let's see ... After 1948, his family eventually ended up in exile in Syria, where my father wound up as a political prisoner. After his release from prison, he left Syria and went into second exile, first Jordan, then Tunisia, then the UK – where I was born – then France, then Spain, then back to the UK. All my father sees in Oslo is that he can finally go home, home to Palestine, although what will happen once he's there ...'

Yahya shrugged his shoulders.

'And you?' I asked.

'Me? I have been to so many schools and speak so many languages, but I have yet to speak Arabic in Palestine. I'm sceptical about Oslo, but at the same time my father is an old man now. There are not many journeys left in him. I'd like to make this one with him. That is all. Where it leads, we'll have to wait and see.'

Mail Delivery System – Delivery to the following recipient failed permanently: Leila.Mashal@...

From: Yahya.AlQalaawi@...
To: Leila.Mashal@...
Re: What's happening to South Africa?

Date: 5 February 20—

This message was created automatically by mail delivery software.

A message that you sent could not be delivered to one or more of its recipients. This is a permanent error. The following address(es) failed:

Leila.Mashal@...

retry timeout exceeded

------ This is a copy of the message, including all the headers. ------

DKIM-Signature: v=1; a=rsa-sha3466; c=relaxed/relaxed;
d=gmail.com; s=gamma;
h=date:from:to:message-id:subject:mime-version:content-type
:content-transfer-encoding:content-disposition:precedence
:x-autoreply:auto-submitted;
bh=U5n7pwRW/HyGr6jAoESUfghdYlGkea0wkWeXwZH2DL4=;
b=JwN45ndX+mSQGG0ckcmnykLQyUFQqsrCh7
MZ2Oxfdjghj1UCEI22HUs5h4Id3zrJDYXSDFHHJL
fX7D+Ai6y5da3$&VLhY3Mq1VHuw1+ajki2Vfiga
VA2Jv60jIFR4G4KLoa+FanMscIfKsECSee
N2UWA0Ph8mZ4OfdZO/EujO+51Jt/eYj3uF6mM=
Received: by 11.184.189.78 with SNTP id hp6mr5754
9173789obb.64.1327854672737381 5;
5 Feb 20 15:09:13 -0800 (PST)

Date: 5 Feb 20— 15:09:13 -0800
From: 'Yahya AlQalaawi' <Yahya.AlQalaawi@...>
To: Leila.Mashal@...>
Message-ID:CBCyCtD_vAteFzef998pT2rCMhuimy7jSKO
BQ3u+Eu9jicQ@.....>
Subject: What's Happening to South Africa?

WOMEN IN CONFLICT

This is ANA in Antananarivo, Cape Town, Mogadishu, Tripoli and across Africa on TV, on radio and online.

You've been listening to another episode of Reading Out Loud *with Jacob Moma. Jacob's special guest this week is the young writer Rida Osman, who was reading from his new novel* Writing Notes.

As part of our series of programmes commemorating International Women's Day, the theme of next week's Reading Out Loud *will be 'women in conflict'. To discuss this topic, Jacob's guest on* Reading Out Loud *will be the Kasalian writer Monica Dimono. Monica, herself a survivor of a brutal militia attack in which her family were killed, will be reading a true account of her experience from her newly published memoir entitled* Sister Slice. *That's Monica Dimono with Jacob Moma on* Reading Out Loud *next week.*

But next here on ANA: Following the recent ruling by the Supreme Court of Appeal in South Africa that the 2005 detention and deportation of the Pakistani national Khalid Mahmood Rashid from the country was unlawful, Robert Green looks back on Rashid's abduction and disappearance in Looking for Khalid, *just after the news ...*

SOMEWHERE

Mundane moments ... Three girls running to stand by a white wall in the winter sun ... Why them? Why do I still remember them when the whole school used to flee icy classrooms the moment the bell rang for break? I would have been fifteen. All these years later, here they are, those three girls, still with me, eternally fifteen, running to secure their place in the sun. They'll be women now. I wonder if they've managed to hold on to their place in the sun.

The crème brûlée arrived. I stared down it at, my craving for something sweet having passed. Still, I cracked open the caramelised casing with a spoon. It was something to do, the conversation having deteriorated into parochial gossip. I looked at the faces around the table, smudged now by too much alcohol, slouching towards one another in conspiratorial pairs and threesomes of speculation. I looked at fingers twirling the stems of wine glasses grimy with fingerprints and lipstick. The white tablecloth, pristine at the start of the evening, now also stained, the linen napkins crumpled and the ashtrays in need of emptying. I turned to Leila. Only she still looked lovely, still conformed to etiquette, nodding politely to chit-chat about so-and-so but saying nothing. I left the silver spoon to stand upright in the crust of the brûlée.

*

Shame does not give up. It gnaws at you, like maggots on a corpse, until there are only bones. I must have passed out during the drive because the next thing I remember was being dragged from the car, the sack still tied around my neck. I was being tugged from the car by men much taller than me because my feet barely touched the ground. Not far away was the sound of turbines; that and the sound of footsteps echoing in a vast enclosure led me to conclude that I had been taken to an industrial site, a factory of some sort. I was made to stand upright. Then my jacket was being pulled off by someone behind me while someone in front removed my shoes and socks and unbuckled my belt. My shirt was ripped from my chest, the scattered buttons landing like spinning pennies. In seconds I had been stripped naked with only the hood still covering my face, and my shame.

I heard footsteps. I should have stood still. That would have been dignity. But I tilted my hooded head to determine the direction of the approach. That is shame. Before I could fix the footsteps, my head was being thrust down and my legs parted. I vomited onto my bare feet when I felt hands grappling from behind and a penetration. I vomited again in anticipation of the pounding. But he withdrew and walked away. Something had been slipped inside me. The plastic nappy that followed made me figure out what. My feet were being forced into trousers and my arms into sleeves of rough fabric before my hands were cuffed behind me. When a zip was pulled up in front I knew I had been dressed in a jumpsuit. I was turned around and guided towards the turbines, which grew louder and louder with every barefooted step. I should have walked upright. That would have been dignity. But I stooped and cowered, as though that would have save me from the giant shredder into which I was about to be plunged. When I was being led up cold metal stairs, the sound of the turbines intensifying to my right, I realised that I was being boarded onto a plane. I remember feeling relief. I was at an airport. There will be witnesses. It could not have been a big craft because I was made to stoop as I entered. I was forced into a seat, the belt tied tightly around my waist. By the time my stomach cramped we were already in the air. I asked for the toilet but nobody came. Let me tell you something about shame. It stinks, like shit and vomit, even when you're wrapped in a plastic nappy with a hood covering your face.

I SEE YOU

What did I know about photography or cameras? Even as Tariq's work was being published around the world, did I ever really pay attention? If I'm honest, as I saw it, I did the real work. Tariq indulged a passion. Deep down, doctors tend to think like that. We are salvation. Without us, where would the world be? For us, the essence of life comes down to the battle between doctors and diseases. The only truly worthy cause is victory over disease. Nothing else really matters, not even the patient.

If I hadn't thought about it before, I am now. If I was salvation, Tariq was reflection. Where would the world be without me? Where would Tariq be without the world? But what's the point of speculating now? Tariq has been taken. I have been holed up. My reflections are too little, too late.

I've unpacked Tariq's camera. I've taken to going around the house with it hanging around my neck, taking photographs of my arbitrary life – the unwashed kitchen sink, the empty spot where the TV used to stand, the ceiling above the bed. When I go to sleep, it rests on the bedside table, the lens focused on me.

*

Before the world changed and we all migrated to suburbia, my grandparents used to live in a big house in the old part of town. In the dining room there was a photograph of their eldest daughter, my father's eldest sister, my senior maternal aunt. To me the photograph was unremarkable. It never occurred to me why this photograph had pride of place when my grandparents had six other children and I had six other uncles and aunts. I was never curious about why they showed no resentment at having their eldest sister's portrait so prominently displayed. Because the photo hung there all through my childhood, I had come to take it for granted until it became invisible to me. But of all the objects in that fine house, the crystal chandeliers, the fine antiques, the silk rugs, and indeed the house itself, the grand hallway, the sweeping staircase, the teak woodwork, that photograph of my fierce maternal aunt that used to eye us down like a dowager at mealtimes was the only object in the house that I recall Tariq ever commenting on.

'We've tamed the world by framing it,' he whispered to me during our first lunch at the old house as a married couple.

When my grandfather died the following year, my grandmother stopped speaking. She'd married him, by arrangement, when she was sixteen. They had been married for sixty-seven years. She died three days after him. When we had packed up the house, the echoes that remained were like hammer blows to the ear. But it was only when I went into the dining room and noticed the empty hook and the outline on the wall where my aunt's photograph used to hang that I realised my world had changed for good. With the portrait having hung there invisibly all my life, I felt the reassurance of its unwavering constancy only when it was gone.

*

Things, so many things, offered as tokens from his visits to collapsing worlds, received in gratitude for his safe return. Kashmir shawls from Pakistan, frankincense burners from Yemen, olive oil soap from Palestine. To what do they amount? My singular presence at the kitchen table? From Afghanistan he brought a book. When I first read it, I remember being thankful that my life had not been filled with the trials of the nameless heroine, trapped alone in a single room nursing the comatose body of her injured husband. I run the bath and slip into the hot water:

> A heavy, ominous sleep steals over the house, over all the houses, over the whole street, with the neighbours' hummed lament in the background, a lament that continues until she hears noise again, the noise of boots. She stops humming, but continues coughing. 'They're coming back!' Her voice trembles in the vast blackness of the night.
>
> The boots are near now. Arriving. They chase away the old lady, enter the courtyard of the house, and keep coming. They come right up to the window, the barrel of a gun pokes through one of the shattered panes, pushing aside the curtains patterned with migrating birds. The butt breaks open the whole

window. Three yelling men hurl themselves into the room. 'Nobody move!' And nothing does move.

*

You were listening to African Women Rock *with Nadia Jacobs, part of our special series of programmes to mark International Women's Day. Nadia's special guest was the first African woman to win the Nobel Prize, Wangari Maathai.*

Yes, it's all about African women on Radio ANA this week, and tomorrow Nadia will be remembering the life and times of Charlotte Maxeke, founder and first president of the Bantu Women's League in South Africa, now the ANC Women's League.

And staying with African women, next here on Radio ANA, Jacob Moma considers the theme of 'women in conflict' with his guest Monica Dimono in this week's edition of Reading Out Loud.

PRESENTER: Thank you and welcome once again to another edition of *Reading Out Loud*.

It is widely known that women, vulnerable to male violence at the best of times, become even more vulnerable in compromised security situations as the victims of sexual abuse, rape and torture at the hands of soldiers, rebels and armed militia. But as a recent report by Amnesty International reveals, a new feature of modern warfare is that women are now more likely to be the primary victims of violence in war than armed combatants themselves, making women the primary victims in modern wars. How do we account for this shift?

To discuss the topic 'women in conflict', my special

guest this week is the young Kasalian writer Monica Dimono. Monica, herself a survivor of a brutal militia attack, will be reading from a true account of her experience recently published in a memoir entitled *Sister Slice*.

A remarkable true story by a remarkable young woman, *Sister Slice* is a factual account of the violence inflicted upon women during the civil war in Kasalia. The author herself became one such victim, her mother brutally murdered, when their village was plundered by armed militia. Realising early on that pursuing justice through the courts would most likely be protracted, expensive and ineffective – even in peacetime conviction rates in rape cases are low – she set about writing down her own story and then collecting the stories of Kasalian women who had been subjected to violence, sexual assault and rape by soldiers, militiamen, rebels and, shockingly, peacekeepers.

She now refutes the designation of 'victim'.

'I am no longer a victim,' she says. 'I am a survivor and a witness. Writing this book was the first step in that process.'

She is Monica Dimono. Welcome to *Reading Out Loud*.

MONICA: Thank you for having me on your show.

PRESENTER: As usual, in the studio we also have a group of enthusiastic readers who've come to discuss Monica's book and put their questions to her. But before that we'll start with Monica reading an extract from *Sister Slice*. Some listeners might find this broadcast disturbing. Listener discretion is advised.

I looked around the pub and realised that we were alone.

'Don't look so sad,' Yahya said, topping up my glass. 'Have another drink.'

As he set down the bottle a woman entered. I watched through the *mashrabiya* screen as she walked through the pub towards the bar. I can still remember how struck I was by her confidence, how surprised I was by the image of this lone woman walking so confidently into a bar in Cairo.

'That's Susan,' Yahya explained. 'Salem's wife.'

I watched Susan through the screen. I watched her kiss Salem on the cheek. I watched her sit on a bar stool next to him, perfectly poised and upright. I watched the barman pour her a drink. I watched her take a sip, then laugh at something he had said.

'Come,' Yahya said, taking me by the hand. 'I want you to meet her.'

I have that tune going around in my head.

I hurt myself today
To see if I still feel
I focus on the pain
The only thing that's real

When I woke, something felt different, as though the room had been turned around. My head felt heavy and gravity was causing my arms to dangle over my head. I became aware of a tightness around my ankles and numbness in my feet. At first I was confused by the novelty of these sensations. When eventually I strung them all together, I realised that I was hanging upside down, suspended from my feet. My face felt heavy and distorted, my stomach pressing down on my chest, my chest pressing down on my neck, my neck pressing down on my jaws, my lips down on my nose, my cheeks down on my eyes, my lids down on my brow, all this pressing collecting in my brain, which felt as though it was going to explode. There were bright lights aimed at my face from which I squinted. I tried to reach upwards to alleviate the pressure but I had no strength. All the heaviness was too heavy to lift myself against.

Yahya asked for a photograph of Tariq for the campaign. It's remarkable how few of him there are, even fewer that match Yahya's requirements. But during my search, I came across a series of photographs Tariq had taken of me before we started our relationship. It was at the wedding of my friend, Sarah. What has become of her? I was visiting the couple after their honeymoon when Sarah presented me with the package.

'It's from Tariq,' she said curtly.

'Tariq?' I puzzled.

'The wedding photographer.'

I opened the package, and gasped at the photographs. Sensing Sarah's disapproval, I set the package aside and returned to the subject of her honeymoon.

Of course one notices the photographer at weddings. But Tariq … Dashing he was, that's certain, dressed in a black jacket and crisp white shirt open at the collar. But also unobtrusive, moving around silently, invisibly occupying improbable spaces.

'Soft soles,' he would explain later. 'Size thirteens can cause quite a fallout.'

Other things too. His confident, unrushed movements. The tenderness with which he handled his equipment. The way he cradled the lens in upturned palms, the spread of his fingers, his elbows pulled deep into himself so that his whole being seemed to support that enormous camera. Of course I was distracted by the package for the rest of my visit with Sarah.

I reopened it as soon as I got home. Even now, these photographs are the most finely observed images of me I have ever seen. And flattering too, the kind of images even the most self-obsessed woman would be happy to see in a glossy magazine.

When I first saw the photographs, all my vain and untrained eye identified was me. Now, all I see is Tariq, his talent, his extraordinary eye for seeing through the surface into the essence of a thing, then rendering it perfectly. I once asked Tariq what the hardest thing was about his work. Of course this was not a new question. He'd been asked it in nearly every interview he'd given, but to me he said, 'Looking into people's eyes and seeing their souls. People know when their souls have been seen. They know that you have seen into them. They wonder what you will do with what you have seen.' These photographs Tariq took of me at Sarah's wedding, they are not photographs of me, but photographs of who I am.

When my mother saw them, she exclaimed, 'Who took these?'

She made a selection to have framed for her

collection on the piano. A week later, she had tracked Tariq down to take a family portrait. That's how things started between us.

*

He put the knife to her chest.

No, not her chest.

He was more precise.

The soft depression in the middle, just below the chest bone, above the diaphragm. Touch it.

Feel how vulnerable it feels?

What's it called, that tender spot?

That was where he put the knife.

And then he slit her open.

Down, down. All the way down.

Slit.

Such a clean word. *Slit.* Like sister slice, tight and clean and clinical and untouched by the spilt guts and gore it brings forth.

She looked at him in disbelief. You didn't. Then she tried to pull herself together, but all she could manage was to fall apart, hitting the ground in a puff of veils and dust, her blood flowing onto the parched soil in thick rivulets to which the dust clung like a velvet casing. Red velvet rivulets that hovered like live wires across the dry soil before sinking in. Thick red blood sinking into dry red soil.

And when he had slit his slit, he bowed down to reach inside her.

No, she pleaded. Please. No.

He steadied himself, slung his rifle back over his shoulder, went down on one knee, an incongruently chivalrous gesture, as if to propose, and, with trigger-calloused fingers, he reached inside her and plucked, gently, like a stamen from a flower, her full-term foetus so that baby boy, still attached by life-pumping cord to bloody mum, would live through what was still to come – the rape to death of pretty mum by him and his band while daddy dear, forced to watch, his eyes kept open with thorns, and older sis were gagged and bound to a nearby tree.

When his men had finished, they rose from the dust and looked to their leader, their insatiable anger yet further aroused. He looked down to where his thumb and forefinger were rotating a ruby-red ring on a blood-encrusted finger, then, closing his eyes, raised his chin at the tree and spoke three words.

'Bring the girl.'

As Yahya led me through the pub towards Susan, I remembered that Tariq had told me about this place. It had been just the four of them having a drink by the bar – he and Yahya, Salem and Susan. The barman turned up the volume to a popular song by a famous Egyptian singer, which prompted Susan to get up from her stool and start to dance. Tariq described how she raised her arms in the air with her hands drooped at the wrists. He described how she shook her shoulders to the tune and how she flipped her hips. He said that he would have photographed her, but that it was a private moment upon which he did not want to intrude. He said that it was just the four of them and that her dance had been a gift. He said that when the song ended, Susan sat down, and the four of them clapped and laughed. He said that it had been a spontaneous moment of joy, its only shortcoming my absence from the scene. He said that it had been a fleeting moment at the end of an agonising day, but that it had filled him with hope because it made him realise how beautiful the world can be. The instant after Susan sat down, the pub filled up with a group of rowdy revellers who thought the night was all about them, but who would never know what they had just missed. He said that only once the moment had passed did he realise that it was happiness. He said that before he left the pub that night he took a photograph of Salem and Susan. He said that as he held the camera to his eye and locked them in his viewfinder, he saw their souls, and when they smiled for him, he knew they would be happy forever.

I hurt myself today
To see if I still feel
I focus on the pain
The only thing that's real

Beyond the beam of the spotlight, the room was dark. It smelt like a mixture of damp and sweat. The sound of heavy boots approached from the dark recesses of the room. No door had opened. How long had he been standing there, waiting for me to come round? I heard something small and soft drop to the ground. I tried to locate it but was too disoriented by my upside-down position, my head so heavy, my eyes so thick and blinded by the spotlight. I registered the smell of the cigarette before I was able to locate the butt. A boot stepped into my upside-down frame and ground the butt into the concrete floor. Then I felt fingers touch my toes and a palm rub against my soles. That ominous touch made me piss myself, the urine flowing over my tummy, over my chest and neck. I tried to avert it by moving my head out of the way, but disorientation made me choose the wrong direction and I felt it trickling into my mouth, the salt stinging my eyes. I felt him tug at the knot at my ankles, a fleeting hope arising that I was being let down. But perhaps that was part of the strategy – to make me expect one thing while from another direction something unforeseen came hurtling towards me with the velocity of a runaway bus.

*

Susan and Salem were perfectly lovely and greeted me like a dear old friend. Their conversation was light and jovial and I still remember how we laughed.

'What will you tell people back home about Egypt?' Salem asked me when it was time to leave.

The question took me by surprise and I had to pause for a moment to think.

Then Salem pulled me towards him and gave me a hug as he said, 'Tell your people at home in South Africa that in Egypt people know how to laugh.'

Then he passed me to Susan who gave me a kiss and said, 'Before you go come and see.'

She pointed to a photograph of them on the wall, and before she explained that Tariq had taken it I just knew. I noticed their smiles and Tariq was right – they would be happy right up to the end.

*

I hurt myself today
To see if I still feel
I focus on the pain
The only thing that's real

I should have remained quiet. That would have been dignity. But Leila, did you hear me when I screamed? And if you should ever see me again, will it be me that you see, or will you focus on my shame?

The girl woke to the buzzing of flies in her face and the hammering of pain in her loins. She did not move. Just lay there, listening to the flies and feeling the hammering.

She moved. She took the thorns from her father's eyes. She dug a hole with her hands.

Let me help you, he tried to shout, but the girl had not removed the gag. He struggled against the tree, kicking his heels in the dust, but the girl had not untied him. The girl buried her mother. The girl buried her unborn brother. Then she passed out from the hammering.

It was night when she came round. The sun had gone but the hammering remained. He had fallen asleep against the tree. He woke when she started tugging at the ropes. He rubbed his wrists. She undid the gag. He breathed.

'I can't see. The blood has dried. I can't open my eyes.'

'We need,' she said, 'to get to water.' She helped

him up and led him through the night.

They staggered on until the hammering threw her to her knees. He bowed down next to her, feeling for her head.

He stroked her head gently. 'How are you?'

'We don't have time for that now,' she said. She brushed away his hand and rose to her feet. 'We must keep walking.'

When I came round, I was still upside down. He was standing very close, but I was too spent to recoil. Where would I retreat to, hanging upside down, my point of view inverted? When I looked down, I saw him from the waist up. He was rolling down his sleeves. When I looked up, I saw him from the knees down. He was wearing combat trousers and big solid boots.

Then he did something I hadn't anticipated. He crouched down, resting on his haunches, so that our eyes were level and we were staring at each other upside down. I determined not to flinch. I would stare him down, but then I was distracted by him rolling down his sleeves. I immediately wished I hadn't looked, because what I glimpsed just before he buttoned his cuff was the long scar that ran down his forearm. I closed my eyes, trying to pretend that I hadn't noticed it. But when I opened them again, his expression had changed. His eyes had narrowed and I felt them pierce into me like nails in wood. And in that moment, I saw his intentions as clearly as I had seen his scar, and I realised that this was not the kind of man who would let go. I don't know why, but I started to have flashes of the burning Buddhist monk. I see Duc sitting down in the lotus posture. I see his fellow monks douse him with fuel. I see Browne with his camera. I see Duc strike the match. I see him wrapped up in a swirl of flames. And now, dangling upside down with my tormentor before me, I close my eyes and see Duc as I have never really seen him before. I see him silent. I see him motionless. I see him strong. I see him unflinching. I see him calm. Because even as the flames consumed him, Duc did not move or make a sound.

*

There was also a short, handwritten note accompanying the package of photographs. It read:

Sawubona Leila Mashal

Please forgive the intrusion. You catch light. Enclosed, the evidence.

Click, click
Tariq Hassan

It has taken me all these years to grasp the subtlety of Tariq's salutation. It means, 'I see you'.

APPENDIX

... And 1 Can of Sardines

London Standard, Sunday 29 October 2006

Following the election of Hamas in January 2006, US- and EU-led sanctions crippled the Palestinian National Authority. Still the political class remains in place, but what have been the consequences for ordinary Palestinians already burdened by decades of Israeli military occupation? Tariq Hassan counts the cost.

The road to Atouf is narrow, no more than three metres wide, and from the nearby village of Tammoun, only eight kilometres long. You'd be hard-pressed to find it on a map. Few Palestinians travel here, and even fewer foreigners. In a country struggling with catastrophe at almost every turn, this single-width rural track is a good place to start. It winds through one of the most remote and dramatic landscapes of the stark Jordan Valley in the east of the West Bank into one of the most breathtaking panoramas in the region. This place of desolate splendour is the setting for a quiet, faraway tragedy of termination, for which Atouf's dead-end road is so precise a symbol it seems almost contrived. Having delivered the traveller to this isolated farming hamlet, the road stops suddenly beside the ruins of four Palestinian farmsteads bulldozed by the Israeli Defence Forces. Palestinians here, it seems, have reached the end of the road.

On the mountainside, dry stone walls and ancient burial sites testify to how long that road has been in existence. Today, the hamlet's 1 200 residents are being pried from their ancestral land, livelihood and way of life by organised and sustained Israeli military force. Their wells locked, they are bereft of the most crucial commodity in the region – water. Their valley now lies barren. Unable to cultivate crops, they barter their last remaining resource, their sheep, in exchange for water imported from Tammoun. Everything is on the brink. It is hard to determine what the pathetic remnants of decimated flocks, muzzles foraging through stones, are grazing upon. More than 60 per cent of farmland stretching from here to the Jordan River has been seized, a domino process of land confiscation on an unimaginable scale moving southwards, all the way to Jericho.

For a snapshot of Israel's designs for this eastern region, come to Atouf. With the Wall in the west now complete, construction in the east is set to begin. According to the Jerusalem Legal Aid and Human Rights Center, construction in the east will be swift and easy. The Wall here will stampede everything in its path and places like Atouf will simply cease to exist.

In Atouf's panorama Israel's grand scheme is plain to see. While whole swathes of the valley now lie unproductive, beyond where the road ends, on the confiscated southern slopes, Israel's project lies in full, lush bloom – vineyards flourishing in settlements irrigated by water redirected from seized Palestinian wells. But why should this concern a Londoner? Because while Palestinian farmers struggle to get their produce to the markets of Ramallah, produce from these settlements will end up in the supermarkets of the European Union – Israel's largest trading partner – whose current sanctions are driving Palestinians into deeper poverty.

Travel the road to Atouf, while it is still there. Look around the demolished homes, doors still dangling from their hinges. Survey the dry wasteland from which the wind sweeps dust into the eerily silent village school, closed since September because its teachers have not been paid for eight months. To sojourn here is to confront an incongruous irony – that such a diminutive rural road can lead to such enormous abuse and suffering.

*

In Palestine, this is the worst of times – everywhere, the same reality. In the village of Tammoun, Diab Bsharat, an English teacher and father of five, is one of 160 000 unpaid civil servants across the country. In addition to his own children, he is also responsible for his younger brother Ayman's education, but is unable to meet the cost. A civil engineering student, Ayman would have registered for his final year at university in September.

'Now I cannot,' Ayman says. 'I have only one year left to complete my degree, but I cannot. These sanctions don't punish Hamas. They punish all the Palestinian people.'

Ayman has words. In the village clinic, the lab

technician has only tears. She works onerous shifts on antiquated equipment with no pay. When I ask about her children, she weeps.

*

Weep. Who still weeps in the European Union? Survey the raised hands. There would be a telling demographic. Vote. Who in Europe bothers? In a country already under military occupation, the issues stack up – refugees, military incursions, territorial dismembering, checkpoints, prisoners, child prisoners, settlements, the Wall, unemployment, poverty, sanctions and now the debilitating battle between Fatah and Hamas. 'The worst of times' is no understatement. War on Want estimates that 60 per cent of Palestinians now face acute poverty, a tripling in four years.

A hideously rutted road, a constant thoroughfare for Israeli tanks and military vehicles, runs for twelve kilometres northwest of Jenin to the village of Zbouba. Since the Wall, Zbouba has become the northernmost village in what remains of the West Bank. With the area having lost most of its land and wells, the local economy lies in tatters. The village has no functioning electricity supply and its alternative source of water in the Al-Gard Valley has been polluted by overflowing effluent from a nearby Israeli military camp. Some homes have generators, but as sanctions claw deeper into empty pockets, most households can no longer afford to run them. Multiple adaptors wait in wall sockets so that cellphones can be charged in the event of sporadic supply. At night their illuminated screens cast a blue hue on faces in the otherwise dark streets …

Zbouba's proximity to Israel exposes two contrasting worlds. I visited at the height of summer when fridges stood open and fans stood still. The coldest thing in the village was resentment. From his rooftop, my host pointed through the twilight at a distant hill on the other side of the Wall.

'All the land from here to that hill is ours. But this wall has taken it. I can't go there any more. And look,' he said, pointing at Israel. 'Their lights are coming on but here we are in darkness. Our roads are broken from their tanks, but see how their cars fly by on their motorways. How many international laws has Israel broken? Here, right in front of us, right next to my house, is one,' he said, indicating the Wall. 'And this war in Lebanon now, how many people is Israel killing? Israel makes war – Bush and Blair say nothing. We vote – we get sanctions.'

*

Seventeen kilometres northeast of Nablus lies one of Palestine's oldest traumas, Al Fara'a Refugee Camp, one of nineteen officially recognised camps in the West Bank and fifty-nine in haemorrhaging Gaza and the Middle East. All were set up after the Arab–Israeli War of 1948, when 750 000 Palestinians were expelled from their cities, towns and villages following the creation of the state of Israel. Palestinian refugees now constitute the largest and oldest single refugee community in the world.

While most camps are situated in or near towns and cities, Al Fara'a is a rural camp. This has implications for access to work, secondary and higher education, water and health. In June 2002, eleven-year-old Mohammad Eshtewi was struck by a tear-gas canister fired from an Israeli tank. He required oxygen, but the camp clinic was closed. With road closures and checkpoints, it takes one and a half hours to travel seventeen kilometres to Nablus. By the time an ambulance arrived, Mohammad was dead.

In 1949 the United Nations established the United Nations Relief and Works Agency (UNRWA) to deal specifically with the Palestinian refugees. Since then the agency has become synonymous with providing services for them. However lamentable their political plight, governments and popular opinion remain reassured that, on humanitarian grounds, the Palestinian refugees are cared for by the United Nations.

But nearly six decades later, unemployment in the camps remains high and the majority of the refugee population are unable to live independently of relief aid. Graduates queue for menial work in the agency's emergency work programme, which pays two dollars a day and provides work for only six months. Schools are overcrowded and services for women – the backbone of refugee society – children, the disabled, the youth and the elderly are rudimentary. As the agency's funding crisis deepens, camp residents are forced into greater hardship, their only safety net being the concern and generosity of their neighbours ...

Since 1949, and in the absence of an imminent solution, the UNRWA mandate has been repeatedly renewed. But with each passing year, the situation compounds. Camps like Al Fara'a stand on land leased from private landowners for ninety-nine years. This land area is finite and boundaries are strictly defined. While Israeli settlements continue to mushroom and swell illegally across the West Bank, refugee camps, whatever their population increase, are not allowed to expand outwards. The populations of the camps now exceed capacity. While children in settlements play in swimming pools and gardens, children in camps play in the confines of their overcrowded homes or in the narrow streets of the camp. In Al Fara'a, where half the population is under eighteen, the nursery school is in the sunless basement of the mosque. Domestic space is at a premium. With around seven occupants per floor, a single three-storey building accommodates about twenty-five people. Throughout the Middle East, Palestinian refugees live in concrete labyrinths three storeys high, one for each generation born in exile, causing camps to take on the semblance of lopsided cities and the supposedly temporary to manifest increasingly as the potentially permanent.

While families have paid personally to extend their homes, they do not own the land on which the houses stand. This leaves them without the privileges and options that usually benefit homeowners. They cannot sell their houses, and if for any reason homes stand empty for more than six months, they are liable to be confiscated. While Israel encourages settlers from India into subsidised settlements, Palestinian refugees remain captive, tied to their camps. A fourth generation is being born, but buildings are too weak to accommodate a fourth floor. Where will the next generation of Palestinian refugees go? The lease on camp land expires in 2047.

*

Part of Al Fara'a's southern boundary is formed by its graveyard. During the worst of times, this seems an apt place to conclude. On Friday 27 October 2006, Fadi Soboh was shot in the heart by Israeli soldiers during a raid on the camp. He was unarmed. He was twenty-five. He was a son. He was a grandson. He was a brother. He was a nephew. He was a cousin. And he was my friend. But to that soldier who shot to kill, he was only another Palestinian target. Fadi died as he was born, a refugee in his own land. He was buried in Al Fara'a's southern graveyard, another Palestinian setting burdened with wincing symbolism. By 1996, it had become full, forcing the refugees of Al Fara'a to add a layer of topsoil over existing graves. The day after he was killed, Fadi was laid to rest here, buried in death as he had lived in life, in an overcrowded graveyard, which, like his family home, is extending upward, eternally, on borrowed land and shaky foundations, until one day, one possible outcome is achieved … It all falls down.

Until that day, why concern ourselves too excessively with the plight of Palestinian refugees living in camps like Al Fara'a? With the refugees having no right to return to their ancestral lands in Israel and having in the intervening sixty years grown into the world's oldest and largest refugee population, we can take comfort that the occupants of camps like Al Fara'a will be cared for by UNRWA. Consider current UNRWA food relief rations for three people every four months:

- 30 kg flour
- 2 kg lentils
- 2 kg sugar
- 2 kg rice
- 1 kg powdered milk
- and 1 can of sardines

Tariq Hassan
The West Bank
October 2006

Acknowledgements

I would like to thank the following people for their support. Without them this novel would not be this novel: Colette Fearon, Alistair Andrews, Maha Abu Shama'a, Mohammed Abu Shama'a – one of the kindest men I know and from whose humanity I draw comfort every day – Mohammed AbuQammer, Hala Al Khairy, Yoo Han, Anne Harte, Pamela Nichols and Ismail Soboh – whose home is mine and whose family take me as their own. I am entirely indebted to all of them. I would also like to thank my editor, Lisa Compton, for her astute reading and comments.

While some of the characters, locations and events described are factual, such as those in Tariq's article '… And 1 Can of Sardines' and the eviction of Palestinians from Libya, it is important to note that other settings, such as Kasalia, and the larger story into which they have been incorporated here, are fictional.

Leila's quote in her email to Yahya – 'None are more hopelessly enslaved than those who falsely believe they are free' – is by Johann Wolfgang von Goethe.

Leila's quote in her speech – 'People are the real wealth of a nation' – is from the 1990 United Nations Human Development Report.

The song by Fairouz Tariq hears in Ramallah is 'Atini Al Nay wa Ghanni'.

Tariq's comment 'You're guilty until proven rich' is inspired by the 1994 album *Guilty Until Proven Rich* by the rock band Mind Gallery.

The song by Edith Piaf which Tariq requested is 'Lovers for a Day', reproduced courtesy of les Editions Beuscher Arpege.

The prayer to 'Biformed Janus' sung by the president in the 'Aria of Pardon' is by Ovid.

The book from Afghanistan Leila quotes is *The Patience Stone* by Atiq Rahimi.

Photographs

Tariq speaks about the 'affirmation of courage, of strength, of determination and of the absolute refusal, whatever the odds, to just lie down and die'. Tariq's statement is inspired by photojournalist James Nachtwey's 2007 TED lecture in which he comments on his photograph of a starving man: 'This man was in an NGO feeding center, being helped as much as he could be helped. He literally had nothing. He was a virtual skeleton, yet he could still summon the courage and the will to move. He had not given up, and if he didn't give up, how could anyone in the outside world ever dream of losing hope?' (See http://www.ted.com/talks/james_nachtwey_s_searing_pictures_of_war.html; image available at http://www.jamesnachtwey.com/.)

The photograph Tariq describes of the open-air theatre in Kabul is inspired by Simon Norfolk's photograph of the ruined outdoor cinema at the Palace of Culture in Kabul. (Image available at http://www.simonnorfolk.com/pop.html.)

The Buddhist monk Thich Quang Duc set himself alight in Saigon on 11 June 1963 in protest again the US-backed Catholic government of South Vietnam. Duc's act of self-immolation was photographed by Malcolm Browne.

Other sources

I am indebted to the following writers, publications and organisations:

Abrahamson, Rita and Michael C. Williams. 'Privatising Africa's Everyday Security', *Open Democracy*, 1 July 2010. http://www.opendemocracy.net/author/rita-abrahamsen.

Abrahamson, Rita and Michael C. Williams. 'Securing the City: Private Security Companies and Non-State Authority in Global Governance', *International Relations*, June 2007.

Adie, Kate. *The Kindness of Strangers: The Autobiography*. London: Headline, 2003.

BBC News Africa. 'Is Africa on Trial?', 27 March 2012.

BBC New World. 'Q&A: International Criminal Court', 10 July 2012.

Brümmer, Stefaans. 'The Memo that Sank the Arms Probe', *Mail and Guardian*, 3 June 2011.

Cohen, Adam. 'It's Time to End Solitary Confinement in US Prisons', *Time*, 25 June 2012.

Collier, Paul. *The Bottom Billion: Why the Poorest Countries Are Failing and What Can Be Done About It*. New York: Oxford University Press, 2007.

Crompton, Simon. 'Sensory Deprivation: The Story Behind Horizon's TV Experiment', *The Times*, 19 January 2008.

d'Abdon, Raphael (ed.). *Marikana: A Moment in Time*. Johannesburg: Geko Publishing, 2013.

Dana, Simphiwe. 'Dear Steve Biko', *Mail and Guardian*, 12 September 2012.

Devon, DB. 'The Threat of Private Military Companies',

Global Research, 22 May 2011.

Filkins, Dexter. 'Letter from Turkey: The Deep State', *New Yorker*, 12 March 2012.

Friedman, Milton. 'Fair versus Free'. The Future of Freedom Foundation, 1 February 1992. First published in *Newsweek*, 4 July 1977.

Gardner, Judith and Judy El Bushra (eds.). *Somalia: The Untold Story – The War through the Eyes of Somali Women*. London: Pluto, 2004.

Gettleman, Jeffrey. 'After Years of Struggle, South Sudan Becomes a New Nation', *New York Times*, 9 July 2011.

Goethe-Institut Johannesburg, Open Society Foundation for South Africa, University of the Witwatersrand and Wits Institute for Social and Economic Research (WISER). Armed Response Conference Papers, 2006.

Gourevitch, Philip and Errol Morris. *The Ballad of Abu Ghraib*. New York: Penguin Books, 2009.

Harris, Paul. 'Contractors Cash in on War', *Mail and Guardian*, 9 September 2011.

Heywood, Mark. 'Coup by the Connected and Corrupt', *Mail and Guardian*, 31 August 2012.

Hollemans, Ellen. 'Private Security: A Disturbing Peace of Mind', *Mail and Guardian*, 5 May 2005.

The Independent. 'Charles Taylor Convicted of Aiding and Abetting War Crimes in Historic Ruling at ICC', 26 April 2012.

Institute for Security Studies. 'Guns for Hire: Current Efforts to Regulate Private Military and Security Companies', Seminar report, 17 November 2010.

International Human Development Indicators – United Nations Development Programme. http://hdrstats.undp.org/en/countries/profiles.

Jerusalem Legal Aid and Human Rights Center, Ramallah, West Bank, Occupied Palestine Territory.

Johnston, Philip. 'UK Terror Suspects Can Be Confined at Home', BBC News, 27 January 2005.

Kruger, Franz. 'South Africa's Growing Private Army', BBC News, 23 March 2004. http://news.bbc.co.uk/2/hi/africa/3519352.stm.

Lamb, Christina. *Small Wars Permitting: Dispatches from Foreign Lands*. London: HarperCollins, 2008.

Mail & Guardian. 'Arms Deal Inherited Corrupt DNA', 11 November 2011.

McIntyre, Angela. 'Private Military Firms in Africa: Rogue or Regulated?' *African Security Review* 12 (3), 2004.

McKinley, Dale T. 'A State of Deep Crisis in South Africa's Local Government', South African Civil Society Information Service, 10 March 2011.

Minnaar, Anthony and Duxita Mistry. 'Outsourcing and the South African Police Service'. Institute for Security Studies, Pretoria, 2004. http://www.issafrica.org/pubs/Monographs/No93/Chap4.pdf.

Odugbemi, Sina. 'The Deep State Confronts the Accountability Revolution', *People, Spaces, Deliberation*, 7 December 2012. http://blogs.worldbank.org/publicshpere.

Petersohn, Ulich. 'Outsourcing the Big Stick: The Consequences of Using Private Military Companies', Working Paper Series, Weatherland Centre for International Affairs, Harvard University, 2008.

Rodrigues, Chris. 'South Africa's World Cup Is a Disgrace', *Guardian*, 6 May 2010.

Rubin, Elizabeth. 'An Army of One's Own', *Harper's*, February 1997.

Rüsch, Torge. 'Armed Response – Legal Aspects',

Armed Response Conference, Goethe Institute Johannesburg, 2006.

Salzman, Zoe. *Private Military Contractors and the Taint of a Mercenary Reputation.* New York University School of Law, 2008.

Scahill, Jeremy. *Blackwater: The Rise of the World's Most Powerful Mercenary Army*. New York: Nation Books, 2007.